the Problem with Being Slightly Heroic

by Uma Krishnaswami

illustrated by Abigail Halpin

the Problem with Being Slightly Heroic

atheneum
ATHENEUM BOOKS FOR YOUNG READERS
New York London Toronto Sydney New Delhi

ATHENEUM BOOKS FOR YOUNG READERS
An imprint of Simon & Schuster Children's Publishing Division
1230 Avenue of the Americas, New York, New York 10020
This book is a work of fiction. Any references to historical events, real people, or real places are used fictitiously. Other names, characters, places, and events are products of the author's imagination, and any resemblance to actual events or places or persons, living or dead, is entirely coincidental.

For information about special discounts for bulk purchases, please contact Simon & Schuster Special Sales at 1-866-506-1949 or business@simonandschuster.com.
The Simon & Schuster Speakers Bureau can bring authors to your live event. For more information or to book an event, contact the Simon & Schuster Speakers Bureau at 1-866-248-3049 or visit our website at www.simonspeakers.com.
Book design by Debra Sfetsios-Conover
The text for this book is set in Centaur MT.
The illustrations for this book are rendered in pen and ink with digital color.
Manufactured in the United States of America
0713 FFG
First Edition
10 9 8 7 6 5 4 3 2 1
Library of Congress Cataloging-in-Publication Data
Krishnaswami, Uma, 1956–
The problem with being slightly heroic / Uma Krishnaswami ; illustrated by Abigail Halpin. — 1st ed.
p. cm.
Sequel to: The grand plan to fix everything.
Summary: Complications ensue with Bollywood star Dolly Singh premieres her new movie at the Smithsonian Institution in Washington D.C., and super fan Dinni and her best friend Maddie present a dance at the grand opening.
ISBN 978-1-4424-2328-2 (hardcover)
ISBN 978-1-4424-2330-5 (eBook)
[1. Best friends—Fiction. 2. Friendship—Fiction. 3. Actors and actresses—Fiction. 4. East Indian Americans—Fiction. 5. Washington (D.C.)—Fiction.] I. Halpin, Abigail, ill. II. Title.
PZ7.K8975Pr 2013
[Fic]—dc23
2012006279

For my students and colleagues
at Vermont College of Fine Arts
—U. K.

Rose petal milk shakes to all those who read this in early drafts. You know who you are, and I love you all. Caitlyn Dlouhy, thank you for making it possible for my characters to dance again, and thanks to all at Atheneum Books for Young Readers.

the Problem with Being Slightly Heroic

Chapter One

KHSV

DINI AND MADDIE, BEST FRIENDS FOREVER, dance around the room in swirls of green and silver, silver and green. Green and silver scarves, skirts, pants, tunics, shoes, and sandals lie scattered all over Maddie's room. Stripy notebooks and pens are heaped on the desk, along with a jumble of jewelry.

Dini is a fan of Dolly Singh, Bollywood movie star extraordinaire, whose signature colors, as everyone knows, are green and silver, silver and green. Dini is a Dolly fan, so Maddie is with Dini. That's how best friends are.

Faster and faster they go. One. Two. One-two-three. One. Two. Back-two-three and forward-two-three and one. Two.

A bangle clatters to the floor. "Oops," says Maddie.

"Just like Dolly," says Dini. They laugh together.

It's true. Dolly does drip jewelry, literally, wherever she goes. She will shortly be scattering her fabulous baubles right here in the Washington, D.C., area when she and her own true love, Mr. Chickoo Dev, arrive for the American premiere of Dolly's latest, greatest movie, *Kahan hai Sunny Villa?* or *Where Is Sunny Villa?* KHSV for short.

Dini quits dancing to hand Maddie's bangle back to her. "Maddie," she says, "I've got something for you." She flings the trailing end of the scarf over her shoulder and digs in her suitcase. "I meant to give it to you yesterday."

A shoe flies out, and a green stripy sock. "Where is it?" Dini says.

"Where's what?"

"This. Look!"

Maddie looks. Maddie screams.

The door bursts open. It's only Gretchen, Maddie's mom. "Everything okay?" she says, looking around the room. Satisfying herself that no one has died, she exits.

Maddie rolls her eyes. Dini shrugs. Of course everything is okay. Screaming is completely justified.

Dini's gift is a photograph, signed and inscribed in glittery ink by Dolly herself: "Salaam-namaste to Maddie, my dearest friend and fan. Hugs and kisses, Dolly Singh."

"Oh!" says Maddie. "Salaam-namaste! Am I saying it right?"

Dini's not always certain how to say things right in Hindi, but little things like language shouldn't get in the way of enjoying a really good fillum, what true fans call these movies. "I knew you'd love it," she says.

"Is that your house?" says Maddie, looking closely at the picture of Dolly. She's dancing in front of a house whose funny-looking shutters give it a blinky look.

"Your house." The words halt the moment and stretch it like a rubber band. The moment gathers itself and moves on, but it leaves Dini a bit stunned. "Um, yes," she says.

The different places in her life are mixing and merging instead of staying firmly on the ground as places are supposed to do. Here, for instance, is Takoma Park, Maryland, a hop and a skip by Metrorail from Washington, D.C., the nation's capital.

And there is Swapnagiri, the little town in the Blue Mountains of south India whose name means "Dream Mountain," and Dini knows that it doesn't disappoint. It's where Dini now lives with her parents, and will live until Mom's grant ends and they all come back to . . . to here.

Here. There. Here. They swirl and whirl in Dini's mind. She tries to shake off the dizzying effect. There is no time for dizziness.

Maddie is talking about how she can't wait to see all those amazing tea-gardens and houses and whatnot in the movie and how dreams can come true, never mind what anyone says, and isn't that just soooo . . . ? She props Dolly's picture up on her bookcase. "There, how's that?"

"Perfect," says Dini automatically.

It is perfect. It is. Dolly looks on top of the world up there, between a penny jar and a tangle of beads.

Maddie dances some whirly-twirly steps that she ends on a sideways freeze with both arms stuck out. She looks like a person who has stepped out of an ancient Egyptian tomb painting.

No-no-no, Dini thinks. That is not it. Not at all.

"I wonder if we find just the right music . . . ,"

she says, trying to sound helpful and hopeful. She turns the volume up, so that Dolly's voice comes pouring into the room. It's a glorious voice, even in this demo audio cut from the movie soundtrack.

"Haan-haan-haan, nahin-nahin!" sings Dolly in a catchy melody that underscores a stirring moment of decision. Dolly's songs have a way of cutting right to the heart of Dini's own feelings, yes-yes-yes all mixed up with no-no.

Maddie circles around Dini waving a rainbow stripy scarf over her head with both hands. The gold accents on the scarf blur as the Egyptian person step turns into a belly dance of some kind. "How's this?" Maddie demands. "Am I getting it? Close?"

"Nahin-nahin!" Dolly sings.

"Try it this way." Dini shows her how to make V-shaped designs on the floor with one foot, then the other, before leaping forward with a hand extended, palm out.

Then back and around
and one more loop,
and back and around
and one more loop, and again

and again, just

one more loop

and—hands together—

sliiiide

to a

stop.

"See?" She is breathless from it. "Want to try? You have to repeat and repeat and slide-slide-slide. It's a pattern." She has studied every single dance move in a dozen Dolly movies to come up with this combination.

For a brief time, there is only the sound of ankle bells and bangles.

This dance sequence needs to be exciting, and dreamy wonderful. But it also needs to be Dolly-ish, which means no Egyptian-tomb-painting steps.

As they go down to dinner, help Maddie's mom put plates out, pour juice, and pick a salad dressing, Dini frets. She can see that Maddie is worried too.

"Did I do it wrong?" asks Maddie anxiously, blocking her mother's attempts to add sunflower seeds to her salad.

"No," Dini says, although she wants to cry, No-no-no! Or does she mean yes-yes?

It is possible that some of Dini's confusion comes from traces of that odd feeling that travelers know as jet lag, which turns night into day and wakefulness into sleep. Maybe some of it is also because her family is scattered about like bits of Dolly's flying finery. Dad came from India with Dini on that long-long-long flight, but he's staying with a friend who runs a B&B a couple of blocks away. Mom, of course, is back in India taking care of the health and wellness of women in her little clinic.

All of which makes perfect sense. So what's the

problem? Dini takes a moody bite of chicken salad and lettuce sandwich with some kind of mustardy spread that Maddie's mom has made from scratch.

She's been looking forward to seeing Maddie again! To planning this dance. To being here for the grand premiere of KHSV. Nowhere in that looking forward was there even a hint of this mixed-up-ness. She tries to recover a squirt of mustard spread that has escaped from her sandwich, but it splats hopelessly onto the tablecloth.

Chapter Two

Worried

THE MAIL SLOT IN THE FRONT DOOR JANGLES while Dini and Maddie are helping to clear breakfast away. A wad of letters falls with a thump onto the hallway tiles.

"I'll go get them," says Maddie. She returns, waving a magazine at Dini.

"Ooh!"

They huddle together over the latest issue of *Filmi Kumpnee: Your Magazine of the Stars.*

"I see that I'll be putting the rest of this stuff away," says Maddie's mom.

"There it is," Dini says. "The grand opening of KHSV. I knew they'd have something about it."

From the "News 'n' Views" column of *Filmi Kumpnee: Your Magazine of the Stars* ("now also online for your quick and EZ access"):

Greetings to all our Dolly Singh fans! Our inside sources bring us word that fabulous filmi Dolly will soon be making her first American appearance, in the grand USA opening of—say it all together now—

Kahan hai Sunny Villa? KHSV for short!

Yes, we have word that this opening will be held at the Smithsonian Institution, an iconic place equal to the famous Starlite Studios in our own city of Bombay.

But take heed, loyal fans. All is not well in Dollyland, because the word . . .
Take a breath. The word is . . .

Worried.

Yes, we are worried about our Dolly. The marathon filming of KHSV has exhausted her. Now, on the brink of her important American movie premiere, she needs loving care. She needs pampering.
She needs rose petal milk shakes.

Do they serve them anywhere in America? Alas, no, our sources tell us.

What-what-what? No rose petal milk shakes? How will Dolly cope with this deprivation?

We may be worried, but we are also watchful. You be watchful too. Watch this spot for the latest revelations in the thrilling saga of Dolly's conquest of the USA.

"I never thought of that," Dini says. "I've never seen rose petal milk shakes in restaurants here. Have you?"

"Will she really fall apart without them?" Maddie wants to know.

"I don't know," Dini has to admit. Who can tell what will make Dolly fall apart? A rattle in a car did the trick once. Who can tell what things, present or absent, might set off an earthshaking reaction in the mind of a sensitive star?

Chapter Three

A Dancing Effect

DINI'S DAD HAS DONE CHAUFFEUR DUTY THIS morning, driving Dini and Maddie to Thurgood Marshall Airport, which everyone still calls Baltimore-Washington International, BWI for short. Now he stands with his arms folded, staring at the arrivals monitor as it gulps and fixes itself, no doubt in acknowledgment of Dolly's imminent arrival.

"There they are!" Dini cries. "Hi, Dolly! Dolly!" The sight of her erases doubt and worry. She is fine. Yes, Dolly is just fine!

Look at her tripping along in her silver strappy sandals, valiantly shouldering an outsize purse. Her feet must be cold in those sandals.

Dolly's own true love, Mr. Chickoo Dev (a.k.a. Chickoo Uncle), follows in her silvery footsteps. He has on his usual charming yet absentminded smile, and he is pushing a cart across the gulf of gray carpeted floor between the Immigration and Customs counters.

Dini and Maddie wave madly, but Dolly is still too far away to see them. If this were a movie, she'd be in close-up by now. But real life, alas, like a badly executed dance, often has pacing problems.

That is one loaded cart. It looks a bit tippy. Dini longs to rush under the ropes and through the customs X-ray scanner and past the form-stamping people. She longs to run to Dolly and Chickoo Uncle so she can offer them a hand or two, and Maddie could run up with her, so that would be four hands in all, a good amount of help.

But there is a counter and that big expanse of floor and the rope. And a forest of forbidding signs saying things like NO ENTRY and TICKETED PASSENGERS ONLY.

And now Dini has a jiggle in her toes and a wiggle in her feet and she can't, can't, can't stay still because Dolly's getting closer. She's smiling at the Customs man and uh-oh! There goes an earring.

Dini clutches Maddie, who is staring at Dolly as if she has seen a vision, which, of course, she has.

"Wow," Maddie whispers. "She's so small."

"I know," says Dini. That fact surprised her, too, when she first met Dolly. It is, of course, unreasonable to expect a movie star to arrive in real life floating across a theater-size screen.

"Whoa!" Maddie cries as a necklace rips loose. "Airborne!"

The Customs man picks up the flying jewels and hands them back to Dolly. He is not smiling.

Kaching! Papers get stamped. *Kachack!*

"That guy's scary-looking," Maddie says, rolling her eyes toward the Customs guy. He is frowny. And big. He towers over Dolly. He is now going through her suitcase, comparing its contents to a list of items on a form.

Dolly taps her feet with beautiful impatience. Chickoo Uncle pats her arm.

"I hope everything's okay," says Maddie.

Dini has been hoping this very same hope. Now, for the first time ever since they became best friends in preschool, she wishes Maddie didn't have this knack for knowing what she, Dini, is thinking.

"I heard they're really tough about security stuff

at airports these days," Maddie says. A few people in uniform begin to drift toward Dolly and Chickoo Uncle, there by the Customs scanner. A small, fearful knot ties itself up inside Dini, climbs into her throat, and settles there.

Chapter Four

"Don't Arrest Her!"

WHAT'S WITH ALL THE PEOPLE IN UNIFORM? They're all milling around next to a sign that says in big letters SECURITY LEVEL: ELEVATED.

Dini does know the meaning of the word "elevated." It has something to do with being up high, like mountains. But what do they actually *do* when the security level elevates itself in this mountainous manner?

"You don't think . . . ," says Maddie, still in mind-reading mode, "that *they* think *Dolly's* a threat of some kind?"

"I don't see why," Dini mutters. She grabs at the rope to calm down. This is real life, not a movie. There is some perfectly simple reason for all those uniformed people. She concentrates on thinking positive—a warm, fuzzy technique in which Dolly is a big believer.

And perhaps, after all, the warm fuzziness works,

because now Chickoo Uncle and Dolly turn and walk away from the Customs screening place.

But this dance has only just begun. Dolly drops a ring. "Oh no!" cry Dini and Maddie together.

Stooping to pick up the ring makes Dolly stop. Chickoo Uncle nearly runs into her. "So sorry, darling," he says.

"No problem, darling," says Dolly. They pause a minute to burble at each other, which is what people do when they are in love. If this were a movie, they'd be singing songs, which is also a fine way to show such affection.

Just then Dolly spots Dini and her face lights up. "Dini, darling!" she calls in her ringing-singing voice. She blows a bouquet of kisses and smacks Chickoo Uncle on the side of his head.

He turns in alarm and lets go of the tippy cart. He tries to recover control.

Too late.

In

slow-

motion

time,

the cart rolls.

International Arrivals
customs

It rolls at an angle along the gray carpet. Then it tips beneath the weight of its bags, spilling them right at the feet of a man who is in a tearing hurry.

The man trips. He falls. He crashes to the ground. He lets out an agonized yowl along with words that make Dini and Maddie exchange quick looks.

"You didn't hear that colorful language," says Dad.

"What colorful language?" Dini says.

Dolly, too, ignores the colorfully worded man. She pats Chickoo Uncle on the shoulder as he struggles to right the cart. Then, instead of walking past the security desk and out of the ticketed-passengers area as well-behaved ticketed passengers are meant to do, Dolly turns toward Dini and holds both arms out to her in an extravagance of come-on-and-hug-me-my-best-of-all-fans. Which Dini is, she is, and only ten feet of carpet now lie between them.

Wait a movie minute. An entire crowd of uniformed people has now descended upon Dolly and Chickoo Uncle. The baggage lies unattended all over the carpet. Chickoo Uncle sputters and blinks. Dolly takes a step back.

"Dini," Dad warns, but she ducks beneath the rope.

She can't help it. It's all too much. She runs to Dolly, just as a silver and green sparkly necklace lands on the floor with a *chan-chan-chan*.

"Dini, wait!" Maddie calls.

"Oh no!" says Dad.

Oh, yes, yes!

Dini does not look back. She runs headlong into the crowd. "Don't arrest her!" she cries. "She's a famous movie star! How could you think . . . ? You don't even know who she is!"

This is the way, the marvelous way, in which Dolly told off the villain in her last great fillum, *Mera Jeevan Tera Jeevan,* or *My Life Your Life,* MJTJ for short. Not the exact words, of course. But the mood, the feeling—Dini lifts them right out of that epic scene.

Everyone turns to look at her. She's frozen the lot of them. They're standing like statues, staring. Some of them with mouths open. But life is not a movie, and the moment transitions to a loud outbreak of—

Gunfire? Thunder?

No, laughter!

Why is everybody laughing?

A slightly nauseating understanding dawns on Dini. All these people—ticketed passengers, uniformed Immigration and Customs Enforcement officers, random passersby—are laughing at her. Even Chickoo Uncle and Dolly are wearing mildly amused looks.

And what's Dolly doing? She's signing a piece of paper for a Customs person. She's signing another paper for someone else. She's signing someone's sleeve.

Autographs? When did Dolly-as-security-threat suddenly become a fanfest?

The story unfolds in tattered fragments. A restaurant worker, a fan, spotted Dolly walking out of the gate. He quickly spread the word. One of the Customs guys remembered seeing a picture of her in the *Washington Post* Entertainment section. Something about the movie opening.

An airport may be big and confusing to travelers, but it is a small world for the people who work there. In this airport, being so close to the nation's capital, they are used to bigwigs. Politicians, financiers, and diplomats are a dime a dozen, and no one pays them much attention. Movie stars are rare, however. The airport staff are not about to turn up their noses at someone who is obviously—just look at her!—the real thing.

Soon they disperse, going back to their duties with their autographs happily in hand.

"Dini, darling!" Dolly says. "It's good to see you again."

"Oh, Dolly," says Dini.

There is greeting and hugging. Dini introduces Maddie to Dolly. Dad welcomes Chickoo Uncle with a hearty handshake. As they make their way to the curb, Dolly chats away, while Dad and Chickoo Uncle begin to talk about something called tea futures.

Dini has no idea what kind of future, singular or plural, may be in store for the tea that Chickoo Uncle grows on his estates in faraway Swapnagiri. What is so interesting about the future of tea, anyway? Dini is far more interested in her own future, which looms ahead filled with uncertainty. And, of course, in Dolly's oh-so-glamorous past, present, *and* future.

"I'm so thrilled that you're going to be opening the film festival," she tells Dolly.

"I'm also very thrilled," Dolly says, waving her

hands and causing the usual shower of silver and green. "And most of all I'm thrilled to see you and to meet your friend Saddie."

"It's Maddie," says Maddie.

"Maddie," Dolly says, with her dazzling smile. "Of course. I utterly, absolutely adore all my fans. You know, it's thanks to Dini that I am here in your great country."

"Yes," says Maddie. "I know."

Now they're both looking at Dini—her best friend in the world and the starriest star in Bollywood, whom Dini has persuaded to come here. Whose grand American opening of her latest, greatest fillum will also kick off a whole week of filmi dazzle at the Smithsonian. Dini begins to relax in this adoring glow. So a little shift in perspective got in the way back at the Customs counter. Maybe Dini danced the wrong dance—but it's over now.

Soon they're all loaded up, Dolly and the girls packed into the taxi along with Dolly's bags, and Chickoo Uncle in the car with Dad. The taxi driver has been given directions. Yes, he knows where the hotel is.

And from here on out everything is going to be just fine. Of course it is. What else could it be? Dolly Singh has come to America.

Chapter Five

Futures

THE CAB MAKES ITS WAY TOWARD THE HIGHway. It begins to drizzle. The driver turns the wipers on. They execute a slow, swishy number as the raindrops trickle down.

"So, are you all ready for my grand opening dance?" says Dolly.

"We're working on it," Dini says cautiously.

"Delightful!" Dolly says. "You must show me."

"You here on vacation?" the cabdriver asks Dolly.

"No, no," she says. "It's my work. The work of my heart and soul."

"Is that right?" The cabdriver turns down a ramp onto a highway flanked by green trees. "Baltimore–Washington Parkway," he says proudly. "Is this your first visit?"

"Yes," Dolly says. "I'm here to meet my public."

"No kidding," says the driver. "Well, it'll clear

up for you. Partly cloudy and mild, it said on the Weather Channel."

Dini does not want to be sidetracked by the weather. "Dolly's a movie star," she says from the backseat, where she's wedged behind two suitcases.

"I'm sorry, what was that?" says the driver. "Can't hear you from back there."

"She's a famous movie star!" Dini shouts. "She's here for a movie opening."

"A grand opening," says Dolly.

"Really?" says the cabbie. "Where are you from, miss?"

"India," says Dolly proudly.

"It's on the nineteenth," Maddie yells from behind another suitcase. "Tuesday."

"At the Smithsonian," Dini adds. "Sackler Gallery. You should come."

"Hey, thanks," says the driver. "I'll bring my wife. We both love Indian food."

"It's a wonderful movie," Dini yells. She hopes he knows he's going not to a restaurant but to the opening of a film festival.

"I'll tell my buddy Tariq," he says. "He's from Bangladesh. You know him?"

"I'm afraid not," says Dolly, "but I love the people of Bangladesh with all my heart, because of course they love my movies with all their hearts."

"He'll be so jealous," says the driver. "Wait'll I tell him I gave a ride to a famous star—what's your name, young lady?"

"Dolly Singh," says Dolly.

"I'll tell him," the driver says. "You going to have refreshments at that opening, Dolly Singh? A little tandoori? And those fried doughnuts in syrup, whaddaya call 'em?"

"Gulab jamun?" Dini shouts.

"Yeah, them. Dee-licious!"

"Naturally, we'll have refreshments," Dolly declares. "The museum has arranged for a caterer."

"It's a great place, the Smithsonian," he says. "They have big festivals and whatnot. I'm sure yours will be just as wonderful."

"It will," says Dolly.

Dini finds herself nodding. "Sure it will!"

Maddie joins in. "I love going there. The museums and the Mall."

"Hey, remember when we went to one of those parades?"

"In second grade!" Of course, of course. "The Folklife Festival."

"With floats and dancers and—"

"An elephant!" they proclaim together.

"Whoa!" says the driver. "An elephant, huh? Now that's a parade."

There is a small silence. Then, "It is entirely possible," Dolly says firmly, "that we'll have a parade as well. With—why not?—an elephant."

Oh. "We will?" says Dini.

"Why not?" says Maddie, fending off a carry-on bag. Did she even hear what Dolly said?

"I've always wanted to be in a parade with an elephant," Dolly says. "The way they wave their trunks is charming. As if they're blowing kisses."

Alternate futures for this grand opening—with elephant, without—slip and slide distractingly through Dini's mind. She tries to say something, but just then the cab turns onto an exit ramp. A large green duffel bag with swirly silver monogrammed initials, *DS*, thumps onto Dini's lap, knocking the air right out of her.

Chapter Six

We Regret

WHILE DOLLY IS CONJURING UP LARGER-than-life images of a parade to her little audience in the taxi, a new crisis has just begun to brew in the peaceful offices of the Smithsonian Institution, that cluster of museums known affectionately as America's Attic.

Mr. Rolando Bayan, program director of educational and cultural events at the Smithsonian, has popped into his modest office on this Saturday afternoon to catch up with paperwork.

An official-looking envelope demands his attention. It is stamped OPEN IMMEDIATELY. URGENT. TIME-SENSITIVE MATERIAL.

It was not there yesterday. It must have arrived after he'd left. He opens it with a bad feeling. One person's urgency is often another person's problem.

A single sheet of paper slips out of the envelope.

Its words sear themselves into Mr. B.'s mind. They are weekend-ruining words.

MEMO

To: Rolando Bayan, Program Director of Educational and Cultural Events, Smithsonian Institution

From: Contracts Department, Distinction Catering

Date: April 8, 2011

Re: Special-event catering request

Our chefs have been invited to join the festivities at the Easter Egg Roll at the White House and must attend a planning meeting there on the 19th. Due to this scheduling conflict, we regret we cannot cater your event. We apologize for the inconvenience and hope you will consider us for other events in the future.

The words of the memo dance before Mr. Bayan's eyes. "Regret." "Cannot." "Conflict."

"What am I supposed to do now?" he blurts out to the empty room. He does not mean to whine. He is a retired marine and whining is simply not allowed.

He braces himself. He'll put his secretary on the job. She'll call every restaurant and caterer in town. Someone else must step up to the task. After all, the Smithsonian is hosting an important cultural ambassador.

He picks up a pen. He writes a quick note across the top of the page: "New caterer?" He does not like to end his notes with question marks, but he has no choice. He looks through the rest of his mail. It's a joyless task.

Chapter Seven

Distraught and Distracted

CUT TO THE PROMENADE HOTEL, THAT BEAUTIFUL building with a redbrick facade, located within easy reach of the National Mall and the Smithsonian. Dad pulls up to the hotel. He and Chickoo Uncle emerge from the car. They are greeted by hotel staff, who push a cart up for Dolly's mountain of luggage.

The cab pulls up. "Whew!" Dini says, practically falling out as the driver opens the door. "I was all folded up in there." She pulls a suitcase out, manages to avoid landing it on her foot.

The cabdriver gives Dolly his phone number ("Just ask for Dave, miss") in case she needs transportation again during her stay. He promises to come to the opening. Then Dolly makes her way into the lobby in her green-and-silver paisley tunic and stylish black leggings, with a scarf to match and a silver earring that is just coming loose.

Dini hums the KHSV signature tune—"Haan-haan-haan, nahin-nahin!"—as she reaches, stretches, and manages to deposit a silver suitcase onto the cart. The suitcase topples back down. Dini scrambles out of the way. She and Maddie try to get the suitcase back up again.

"Careful," Dad warns.

"We're being careful," Dini protests.

"Where are we going to find an elephant?" Maddie says.

"I don't know," snaps Dini. She does not mean to snap. It just happens.

"Why don't you two dancing divas go talk to Dolly?" Dad suggests.

That is the first good suggestion Dini's heard in a while. "Okay."

"Stunning," says Maddie. Maybe she didn't get the snappiness. Dini hopes she didn't.

In a quick *chan-chan,* there they are at Dolly's side. At this instant the word "stunning" is a perfect fit for Dolly. Her hair is stylishly disarrayed, slipping out of its silver filigree barrette. She settles into a handy sofa and kicks off her silver strappy sandals.

THE
Promenade
HOTEL

And Dini notices something. Dolly's presence is sending all the male hotel staff into a dithering spin. Five of them now advance simultaneously to ask how they may help her, never mind anyone else present. Dini has always wanted to be like Dolly, but she's never noticed this particular Dolly effect before. She tries to see herself sending boys into disarray like that and fails. Just the thought makes her feel a bit funny.

"Dolly, darling," says Chickoo. He murmurs something Dini can't hear, then says, "They need it so they can check us in."

"Of course, Chickoo," Dolly says, and opens up her purse. She looks inside. She rummages. And looks. She clicks her tongue, shakes her head, wrings her hands. Such cinematic gestures. What is she looking for?

Chickoo Uncle takes a step forward, then stops. Step. Stop. "Take your time, Dolly, no rush," he says. Dini notices that when he's worried, his face is all nose, not to be mean or anything.

Dolly throws up her hands, sending rings flying around the well-appointed lobby. "I know I put it there!" she cries.

"What is it, Dolly?" Dini says, wondering if she should go pick up that jewelry. "What are you looking for?"

"My passport!" Dolly exclaims, knocking all other thoughts right out of Dini's mind. "It was here in my handbag and now it's gone!"

"Oh no!" Dini and Maddie cry in one voice, a voice of alarm and concern. This is serious.

"Let's all stay calm," Chickoo Uncle urges.

"Hold your horses," Dad agrees.

"I think I need a rose petal milk shake," says Dolly weakly.

Chapter Eight

Looking for Rose Petals

DINI AND MADDIE TRADE GLANCES. RIGHT on the money, those *Filmi Kumpnee* people. When Dolly's stressed, she needs her rose petal milk shake.

"Rose petal?" says the hotel manager in alarm. "Hmm, I don't know. I'll go check with the kitchen staff."

Dolly frowns. She looks doubtfully into her purse as if a rose petal milk shake might appear there. How is it, her pained look seems to ask, that such a beautiful hotel cannot summon up this most basic refreshment?

"With chocolate sprinkles," Dolly adds.

"Rose petal, of course, yes," says the manager hastily. "I'll just—that is, I'll see what I can do. And chocolate sprinkles? A round of that . . . for you girls as well?"

"Yes, please," Dini and Maddie say together.

Maybe the *Filmi Kumpnee* people were wrong. Maybe, after all, Washington, D.C., can step up to the task of keeping Dolly happy.

The hardworking manager of the Promenade Hotel hurries out the revolving door. His honest face wears a worried cast. The source of this worry is the chef in the kitchen of the Promenade Hotel's popular and well-reviewed Urban Delight Restaurant. How is Armend Latifi, creator of gourmet delights and supreme commander of the kitchen, going to react to this new and highly unorthodox milk shake recipe?

Chapter Nine

Possibility

> **NOTICE**
>
> **The Elephant House is closed for renovation. We will reopen April 23 with a new barn, wading pool, and rock-faced run.**
>
> **Thank you for your patience.**
>
> **—Administration**

WHILE DOLLY IS DISTRAUGHT AND DIStracted upon her arrival in America, the National Zoo is winding down from a busy afternoon. The giant pandas are polishing off their dinner of bamboo leaves in their water-cooled grotto. The baby giraffe is pooping a shower of small dung pebbles while its long-necked mother bats her eyelashes in admiration. Assorted children, trying to escape their caregivers, are running in circles around a refreshment stand. A hornbill chick has emerged from its nest and is flapping bravely about the aviary while a researcher with a video camera tracks its wobbly flight.

Meanwhile, near the Elephant House, workers in hard hats have spent the entire day pouring concrete mix into preformed molds. Others have shaped a giant pool; still others have graded a meandering trail. People with tools and bags have been walking in and out of the building all day, fixing wires and moving things around.

Evening falls. From within their ample quarters, the elephants watch the quiet descend. All but young Mini, who has been secluded in the outer pod for a few days on account of a cold. Now she is out in the yard, where she's not supposed to be. She has found something interesting in a brown paper bag.

One of the humans didn't finish his lunch. Perhaps it was the same one who kept going in and out all day long, putting that door up. That shiny new door that swung so conveniently open when Mini nudged it. Not at first, although she could feel something clicking and tumbling about. The third try did it. Third tries are like that.

Mini sneezes, partly from her cold and partly from

excitement. She explores the bag with the delicate tip of her trunk. Little treasures tumble out. Ooh! Crunchy deep and roasty delicious. Mini tucks the morsels one by one into her mouth.

She stays out in the elephant yard for a long time, lost in a peanut daze. Her eyes close. She sways in the gentle spring drizzle. She lifts one foot, then sets it down again. She can tread as lightly as a feather when she feels like it.

If elephants dream, Mini is surely dreaming. Dreaming of peanuts and more. Dreaming some ancient dream stored deep within her elephant memory. Dreaming of wandering free, stripping young leaves off the branches of trees for a snack. Of the promises held by the great wide world.

She flaps her ears. She twitches her trunk. Possibility is indeed a marvelous thing.

NOTICE

Due to rewiring in the Elephant House, all computer systems in this building will be down for 24 hours, effective 8 a.m. on Saturday, April 9.

Thank you for your patience.

—Administration

Chapter Ten

When Something Falls

CABDRIVERS ARE THE EYES AND EARS OF A city. They go up and down and around all its streets and byways, knowing just how to get a passenger all the way from Anacostia to Adams Morgan without being snagged in a traffic jam. They know which streets turn unaccountably into one-ways at certain times of the day, yet open up to traffic in both directions at other times.

Cabdrivers notice things on the road. It is their job to do so. But sometimes they do not notice the things that fall out of their cabs. Especially things that slip out of large purses carried by famous, if slightly careless, movie stars.

So after the cab has driven away, the thing that has fallen out lies there on the sidewalk outside the airport.

Anyone can pick it up.

Chapter Eleven

Bad Pacing

ROOM 503 IS MODESTLY NAMED. A PLUSHLY furnished suite on the fifth floor of the Promenade Hotel, it is tucked away at the end of a carpeted hallway. In the back, sliding glass doors open onto a spacious balcony with a view of the rose garden. Sprawling below is a panorama of woods and streets, parks and houses and shops. A creek cuts a silvery path to the Potomac River. Toward the western horizon the well-trafficked Beltway carries its load of cars and trucks and vans and buses to and fro, to and fro.

To and fro is also how Dolly is pacing at this moment. "Where could it be?" she cries. "I've looked everywhere!" She is speaking of the passport, of course. A purse and a couple of carry-on bags have been turned inside out. Their contents spill over a desk, a coffee table, and a carved wingback chair.

Chickoo Uncle clears his throat. "I think I'd better go back."

"To the airport?" A small glimmer of hope breaks through Dolly's gloom.

"Just to take a look," he says.

"Do you think . . . ? Oh, Chickoo!" cries Dolly, echoing her KHSV character, who began to regain hope after tragedy in just this way.

"Dolly," says Chickoo Uncle, stepping up to his role, "don't you worry."

"Oh, Chickoo, how can I not?" Dolly returns unexpectedly from filmi to real. The switch causes Chickoo to flinch, but Dini can see that he's holding his ground.

"I feel . . . restrained!" Dolly wails. "Restricted. Impeded and inhibited without my passport. Maybe they won't let me leave to go home! How can I make it through the opening with this big worry hanging over my head?"

Her voice rises steadily, threatens to fly right off the edge. Dini's sure she can hear the light fixtures rattling from the vibrations. "Maybe someone found it," she ventures.

"That's terrible!" Dolly cries. "A stolen passport

is much worse than a lost one, no? A hundred times worse. A thousand times, ten thousand!"

Dini has to admit she's a little foggy on the matter of lost versus stolen passports. "Can't we get you another one?" she asks.

"I should think so," Dad pipes up, "from the embassy. But it's Saturday now, and late, so they'll be closed." Which is not, after all, quite so helpful. Dini can see he's trying, but reality has a way of bungling up the best intentions. It's Dolly's song all over again—yes-yes-yes, no-no.

Chickoo Uncle takes both Dolly's hands in his. "Dolly, meri jaan, can you remember when you saw it last? Where?"

Dolly wrinkles her fine brow in the effort to remember. Dini finds herself doing some brow wrinkling too, in sympathy or admiration, or both.

"That Customs place," Dolly says at last. She thinks maybe she left the passport at the counter, or maybe it fell out of her purse on the way to the curb.

"It'll show up," Maddie says. "I bet the people at the airport are holding it for you."

"Maybe they have a lost and found," Dini agrees.

She wishes she could do something real to help, but right at this moment she can't think what. The nasty thought assails her of someone stealing that passport—maybe even pretending to be Dolly . . . and . . . and . . . Dini forces that thought out of her mind.

Maddie gives Dini a look that says, clear as clear, This is not good, what I'm thinking.

"Come on, I'll take you to the airport," Dad says to Chickoo Uncle. "Let's go. We're burnin' daylight here."

"Why's your dad talking like an old cowboy movie?" Maddie whispers.

"He's been reading Westerns," Dini explains. "Cowboys and lawmen and stuff."

"In India?" says Maddie.

Dini rolls her eyes. Who would believe it? In Swapnagiri in the Blue Mountains of south India, Dad found a stash of old Westerns once willed to the library by an American expat tea planter, now regrettably deceased. Dini waits to see if Chickoo Uncle gets the obscure idioms that so delight Dad.

But, "Ha, ha! Burning up daylight. Very clever,"

says Chickoo Uncle, apparently needing no translation.

They march out, Dad and Chickoo, on their heroic errand. Well, marching would work, or perhaps saddling up a couple of fine horses and riding off into the sunset.

In truth, they neither march nor saddle. They stroll out of the room, which is very bad pacing. Real life could be a filmi dance, Dini thinks, if only people could get their movements properly in sync.

Chapter Twelve

Who Will Bake the Cake?

JUST IN TIME (BECAUSE DINI IS STARTING TO feel a bit dizzy from watching her), Dolly quits pacing. This is because her phone has begun to sing. Yes, that is correct. Dolly's phone does not ring. It sings, Haan-haan-haan, nahin-nahin! Dolly's ringtone is a syncopated strings-and-synthesizer version of the lead song from KHSV.

"Yes?" says Dolly, pulling herself together as she answers the phone. "Who's that? Oh, Mr. Mani!" She gestures to the girls to sit, sit. "It's only Mr. Mani," she tells them.

"The baker," Dini explains to Maddie as they perch on the edge of the green velvet sofa. "From Dreamycakes Bakery."

"Oh yeah, the one who's scared of monkeys." Maddie catches on fast. Dini has told her all about the owner of Dreamycakes Bakery in Swapnagiri, a fine pastry chef who yearns for fame and glory and has nightmares about marauding monkeys getting in his way.

"I didn't quite hear that," Dolly says on the phone.

Mr. Mani's voice spills out of the cell phone in an inaudible hum, across thousands of miles.

A pause. Dolly takes a breath. Then, "You mustn't think of it," she says. "Of course you must go to London for your shake-off. By the way, what's a . . . ? Oh, *bake*-off. Yes, of course you must go bake off, Mr. Mani." She listens, then says, "Yes, I know. It's your baby. I do . . . understand. Bye." She clicks the call to an end and sets the phone down.

"Good news," she says, but is that a quiver in her voice? A shiver? A shake? Because her face is not registering good news.

"Tell us!" Maddie cries, clutching at the soft arms of the green couch.

The good news is that Mr. Mani has made it into the *Guinness World Records* in the extra-large confections (with chocolate and floral ingredients) category. He was calling Dolly to apologize. That is because, like the ointment with a fly in it that Dini's dad sometimes likes to go on about, there is a bad-news part to this good news. Mr. Mani can't attend the American premiere of KHSV. He has been invited to London for a demonstration bake-off using the secret recipe that has been in his family since the time of his great-grandfather.

"My grand opening!" Dolly is pacing once more, to and fro and back again. "He was going to bake a cake for it. With rose petals and everything."

Here it is again. Yes and no pulling in opposite directions in a great tug-of-war. How wonderful that Mr. Mani's cake has earned him fame and an invitation to take part in a ritzy-snazzy bake-off demo. How terrible that there's now no cake for the KHSV grand reception.

"It's all ruined," Dolly says, parting ways with an earring. "So many hopes and dreams. So many fans I'm going to let down."

"Oh no!" says Maddie.

"Oh, Dolly," says Dini.

The tension is broken by a knock on the door. Maddie answers it.

"Room service." The rose petal milk shakes have arrived.

Dolly says, "What could I say? He says to me,

'That cake recipe is my baby! The chance of a lifetime. You'll understand.' I tell you, what could I say?"

"A baby?" says the room service man, setting down the tray with the milk shakes. "My wife's going to have one. Our first. Oh, I'm so nervous."

"Dolly, we still have time," Dini says, offering her a milk shake.

"I'm learning to breathe," says the room service man.

"It's just too much," Dolly protests. "First the passport and now this." She clutches the milk shake with a strangled cry, like a drowning person clutching a life raft, or possibly like someone who has swallowed her tonsils.

"So who's having the baby?" says the room service man.

"What baby?" Maddie says. "Whose baby?"

Dolly sips the milk shake and begins to revive. "Nobody's," she says. She still sounds a bit strangled, but her tonsils seem to be wandering back to where they belong.

"An orphan?" Maddie says, alarmed.

"No, no, no," says Dini, sinking back into the

couch. "*Nobody's* having a baby. Dolly was talking about Mr. Mani's cake."

"No baby?" says the room service man.

"But who will bake the cake for my reception?" demands Dolly.

"A cake?" says the room service man. "Is that all?" He accepts Dolly's tip and leaves, disappointed.

"This is great," Maddie says, and hurries to add, "the milk shake, I mean."

"Yes it is," Dolly admits.

Dini sips hers. It's delicious. A little different from Mr. Mani's but very good.

Surely the very good milk shake is a sign. The story will turn. Dad and Chickoo Uncle will find that pesky passport, and then they'll just have to find someone who can bake a really nice cake.

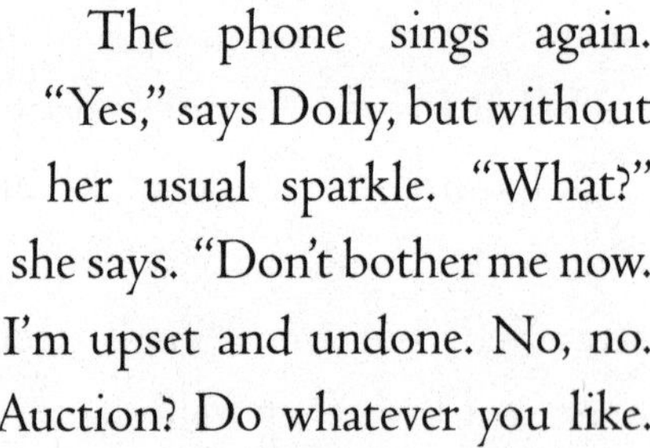

The phone sings again. "Yes," says Dolly, but without her usual sparkle. "What?" she says. "Don't bother me now. I'm upset and undone. No, no. Auction? Do whatever you like. Am I giving you permission? Of course. Auction the thing, whatever it is. Why not?"

She hangs up. "Why are so many people bothering me about so many things?" she says plaintively. "What time is it? Is it lunchtime?"

It is way past lunchtime. "Dolly, shall we get you something to eat?" Dini asks.

"Just a little something, if you don't mind," Dolly says. "I'm too tired to go down."

Dini leaps up. "Sure," she says. "Coming, Maddie?"

"Thank you, my darlings," says Dolly. She clicks her cell phone on again. "Soli? Are you there?"

She's calling Mr. Soli Dustup, the manager and owner of Starlite Studios, far away in India.

From the way Dolly carries on talking, it's clear that she has been unable to reach Mr. Dustup. A person talking to another person sounds very different from one who is doing the necessary but distasteful thing, leaving a voice mail message.

Dini and Maddie talk their way down in the elevator and out the front door. "I have an idea," Dini says, "about that cake."

"What? Tell me."

"Why can't they make it right here, in this restaurant?"

"Sure. If they can do rose petal milk shakes . . ."

"Let's ask them," says Dini.

"Stunning idea," says Maddie.

Through the rose garden and around the hotel they go, until they come to a small door all the way in the back. Dini tries it. Closed. Feels locked.

"Are you sure this is the kitchen?" she says.

Maddie says, "Yup. Back door. If we go the other way, they'll just make us sit down and take our order, right? We need to go back in the kitchen to talk to someone."

"Good thinking," says Dini. She herself never knows which way to turn to get somewhere. Maddie's so good at finding her way around, it's like she has a compass in her brain. That is useful, as there are so many things to find just now—a cake, a passport, an elephant. It is all quite dizzying.

"Mmm, smell that?" Maddie says. "That's the kitchen, all right."

Delicious scents curl and waft out into the air. Something frying. Onions? Potatoes? And something tomatoey. Food. Now voices sound from behind the door, accompanied by the clatter of pots and pans. Definitely food.

"I'm starving," Dini says. "Aren't you?"

Maddie nods. "Stunningly starving," she says, which makes them laugh. They laugh together, and Dini finds she is unable to stop. Laughter takes over her whole body, so she's doubled over from it, and she thinks she may be crying next.

Okay. Enough. Oh! She collects herself. She takes a breath. She knocks-knocks-knocks sharply on that closed, locked door.

Chapter Thirteen

A Little Nervous

IN THE KITCHEN OF THE PROMENADE HOTEL'S Urban Delight Restaurant, where Chef Armend generally rules with an iron ladle, the pace is more relaxed than usual. This is because the chef with the volatile temper and the exacting standards is away. He is in Chicago at a culinary convention, whose attendees he is at this moment probably terrorizing. As a result, Dolly's order of rose petal milk shakes was peaceably processed, much to the hotel manager's relief.

Now, during the dinner shift, the phone rings merrily. Room service orders come in at a brisk clip. Alana, the sous-chef, calls them out as she stirs the soup du jour—cream of fennel—while turning off the oven at the same time so the rolls don't burn.

Despite her fancy title, Alana is what people in the everyday world would call an assistant, but today she is in charge. When the knock sounds, she calls, "Get it, Ollie," without missing a stir.

Ollie opens the door. Two girls dance in.

"Sorry," Alana says, "restaurant entrance is that way."

But the girls aren't leaving. One of them swishes her ponytail in a take-charge kind of way. The other one sticks close to her, in the manner of infantry backup.

Ollie suspects the ponytail swisher may be a sort of junior Alana. An Alana on training wheels. The world needs such people, to be sure, but they make Ollie a little nervous.

Chapter Fourteen

The Real Surreal

"COULD WE GET SOMETHING TO EAT?" DINI asks. "Room five oh three?"

"Call room service." The woman in the chef's hat sounds annoyed. "They'll take your order."

She waits for them to leave, but Dini's not done. Not yet. "And three rose petal milk shakes," she says, adding, "Please." She does not mean to be unpleasant, she's just hungry. Her stomach is sending growly signals to her brain.

"Ah," the woman says, "you're the ones with the milk shake order. How'd you like those shakes?"

"Great!" say Maddie and Dini together.

Maddie says, "Dolly's the one who needs those milk shakes."

"Dolly? Are you Dolly?" She turns to Dini.

"No," Dini says. "Dolly's a movie star. She's totally amazing."

"But jet-lagged," says Maddie. "And tired. And she just lost her passport."

"Alana, I heard we had a famous movie star in five oh three," says the guy unexpectedly.

"No kidding." Alana appears to decide that Dini is mostly harmless. "Okay," she says, "so what do you want to eat with those milk shakes?"

The sidekick gulps. "But, Alana . . ."

"What?" she snaps.

"Chef. Chef Armend. He doesn't like it when—you know . . ."

"Guests wander into the kitchen to place orders?" she demands. "Yes, I know. But, Ollie, I don't see Chef here right this minute. Do you?" Leaving him to battle his weak knees, she turns to Dini. "So? Know what you want?"

"Some of that soup," Dini says. "But can you add some more spices? Dolly likes her soups spicy."

"I'll have some too," says Maddie. "Not too spicy. And a grilled cheese."

"Grilled cheese for me, too," says Dini. "Can you grate a little chocolate into the soup?"

Ollie stares at them as if his eyeballs are about to pop out of his head.

"Move it, Ollie," says Alana briskly. "There's a bag of rose petals in the fridge." She turns to Dini with interest. "Did you say chocolate?"

"Just a little." Dini tells her about Mr. Mani, that talented pastry chef in faraway Swapnagiri who puts a little touch of chocolate into everything he makes, including curry puffs.

"In-teresting," Alana says.

"I don't know, Alana," Ollie says, tripping over his feet between fridge and counter. "He'll be—you know—back on Monday."

"Who?" says Dini.

"Chef Armend," says Ollie, as if she's supposed to know that. "What's he going to say?"

Alana looks at Ollie as if he's an inchworm peering up at her from a head of cauliflower. "Monday," she says, grating chocolate into the soup with energy. "Yeah. Well, there's a whole day between now and Monday, Ollie. Prep those shakes!"

She spoons some soup into a smaller pot, dusts it with powdered ginger. She considers it, then adds cayenne pepper and cumin. "There," she says, "now it's curried fennel soup, woohoo! With a secret ingredient."

Ollie gets to work. "Chef's not going to be wild

about rose petal milk shakes." Or curried fennel soup with secrets. He does not say that, but the thought works its way into the chrome and tile kitchen and hangs in the air.

The blender whirs sweetly. "Wild?" Alana says over the sound of the motor. "I think wild is exactly what he'll be."

They are looking at each other in a sparky kind of way. Dini tries to assess that sparkiness. Is it love in the air, or is Alana going to rap Ollie on the side of the head with a spatula? It's hard to say. Could go either way.

Dini hesitates. Should she mention the cake? She decides to forge ahead. "There's one more thing," she says. "We need a cake."

"Now?" Ollie squawks, splattering milk shake onto the counter.

"No, on the nineteenth," Dini says.

"For the grand opening of Dolly's movie," Maddie explains.

Ollie and Alana are back to looking at each other again in that is-it-love-or-not way.

"So?" Dini urges. "About the cake . . ."

They say together, "We'll have to ask Chef Armend."

Outside and on their way back, Maddie says, "That chef must be a scary kind of guy."

"No kidding," Dini says. "Sounds surreal, if you ask me."

"Totally surreal," Maddie agrees.

Surreal. It's a word they both learned from a DVD special interview with Dolly. She said the movie business was that way. Beyond real, kind of super-real, which is what Dolly herself is, for sure. Really, Dini has to admit, it is quite surreal to think that she, Dini Kumaran—girl who loves movies but still in other ways an ordinary, everyday kind of girl—is now friends with a Number One Star like Dolly.

But surreal could be good, after all, she thinks, with the dance in rhythmic step and the sound pleasingly pitched and lights transforming ordinary into magical. This could be the real surreal.

Chapter Fifteen

Urgent

From: recall1438@trustuswithyourlife.com.us

To: kvincenti@ntnlzoo.si.educ, supply@ntnlzoo.si.educ, admin@ntnlzoo.si.educ . . . and 24 others

Subject: Recall Notice

Date: Friday, April 8, 2011, 18:23:12 EDT

Status: !! Urgent

Please confirm receipt of Recall Notice #05B76T8, attached.

Remember, workplace security is your friend!

From: recall1438@trustuswithyourlife.com.us

To: kvincenti@ntnlzoo.si.educ, supply@ntnlzoo.si.educ, admin@ntnlzoo.si.educ . . . and 24 others

Subject: Recall Notice

Date: Saturday, April 9, 2011, 18:36:01 EDT

Status: !!! Very Urgent

Please confirm receipt of Recall Notice #05B76T8-2, attached.

Item summary: One (1) industrial-strength multilevered lock for interior-exterior installation.
Recall issue: Erratic performance under field conditions.
Remember, workplace security is your friend!

Chapter Sixteen

Terrible Option

BACK IN THE DELUXE SUITE AT THE PROMenade Hotel, Dad and Chickoo Uncle are back from their quest. They sit across from each other wearing mournful looks. The lamp throws their shadows against the wall, so that Dad's glasses and Chickoo's nose take over. Dolly is staring at that wall as if she expects it to fall down. The conversation proceeds in short clips.

Chickoo Uncle: "We couldn't find it. Looked everywhere."

Dad: "Impossible. Needle in a haystack."

Dolly: "Is it lost? Or stolen?" She looks as if she is weighing the options and finding them equally sickening.

What kind of dance includes passports and haystacks? Dini's life is starting to feel like a piece of bad choreography.

"Trail ran cold," Dad says.

"We filed a police report," Chickoo Uncle adds. "They took down all the details."

"The whole kit and caboodle," Dad confirms.

"Called the Indian embassy. Left a message. Called the Smithsonian. Left a message."

Lost passports and grumpy chefs and now Dini has to find an elephant—all these intrusive things are going to edge the grand opening right offscreen.

Maddie is waving her hands inches from Dini's nose. She's loud-whispering, "Dini. You're not listening."

Dini snaps back to here and now. "Sorry. What did you say, Maddie?"

"We can't give up," says Maddie. "We have to do something."

Dini stares at her.

"We have to," says Maddie stubbornly.

And underneath the set of her chin, behind the stubbornness, Dini can see hope and a kind of I-am-here-for-youness. And something else. Maddie is looking sure that Dini will get them all out of this jam. Which is crazy, plain crazy, because what on earth does Dini know about finding lost passports? Or elephants, for that matter? Precisely nothing.

The thing we call coincidence is big in Dolly's fillums. It is neither good nor bad. It just is. Sometimes two people just happen to be in the same place. Their paths cross, whether or not they both know it.

Unknown to Dolly and her supporting cast, someone finds that passport lying facedown on the curbside at the airport (which locals call BWI or sometimes, affectionately, Beewee). Finds it. Picks it up. Looks at it. And then, instead of turning it in to the proper authorities as a well-behaved traveler should do, that someone pockets it and moves on.

In this place where everyone is in a hurry, the stream of people flows around and past that person, who disappears into the crowd.

Chapter Seventeen

Juggling and Jostling

DOLLY HAS STOPPED PACING AND IS SITTING in the wingback chair with a frown on her face. Dinner has arrived and been signed for. "Should I divide up the food?" Dini asks. Looked like plenty when they were in the kitchen. She doesn't know about anyone else, but her stomach is sending her distress signals.

"Good idea," Dad says.

Dini finds a bag of microwave popcorn in a cabinet in the little kitchenette of the suite. She takes a sniff. "What do you think?"

Maddie agrees that on a fresh-to-stale scale it will do. Soon the fragrance of buttered popcorn fills the air, together with the *pop-pop-pop* of kernels.

"Smells good," Dini says.

Maddie brings out cups and glasses, dishes and silverware. "This hotel has everything," she says. "I wouldn't mind living here."

"As in always? I don't know about that." Dini does not want to add any more places—even nice ones like this hotel—to her mental map.

Dolly is not distracted by these minor location digressions. She twists the rings on her hands. "What a bad beginning. An insidious incident. What a terrible turn of events."

"Dolly worries about omens," Chickoo Uncle explains.

"Obnoxious omens," Dolly says, which seals any notion that she might take joy in simple pleasures like popcorn.

Dad divides up the sandwiches and soup. A bowl on the side contains tiny croutons, to which Dolly helps herself liberally. Popcorn makes a reasonable topping for the rest of them, although Dini has to eat it fast, before it turns to mush.

"Not enough salt," Dolly says, adding a generous sprinkling from the shaker. She downs one of the three rose petal milk shakes, so that the rest of them have to share the other two. "I'll just have water," Dad says.

"I'll share a milk shake," says Dini.

"Wouldn't hear of it," Dad says. "Nothing like water."

Dad pours himself a glass of water from the faucet, while questions pour into Dini's restless mind. Did Dolly notice them all doing things for her? Does she ever notice when people go out of their way for her? Bring her dinner—just one small example. But then she thinks, Dolly's not an ordinary person. She's a star. Stars are used to getting their way, and what's more, this is a stressed-out star who has just lost her passport.

"We should have ordered more food," Maddie whispers.

"Oh." At once Dini's petty, ungenerous thoughts subside. Maddie's right. Dini realizes something else. They ordered for Dolly and for themselves. They forgot all about Dad and Chickoo Uncle.

"We can help you unpack," she says, trying to be a better person. They're done eating, and the empty tray has been set outside the door. "You know—if you don't mind."

"You're too sweet, you lovely girls," Dolly says, getting up and shaking out the folds of her scarf. "Come. I'll show you the new jewels I got for the grand opening. Chickoo, where's that suitcase?"

Chickoo Uncle finds the suitcase, which cheers

Dolly up a bit. She pulls out a silver necklace with red-and-green stripy decorations and lets the girls try it on.

"Wowie, wowie!" whispers Maddie in awe.

Dini's speechless, which doesn't happen often. Dolly. Is letting them. Try. Her jewelry. On. How surreal is that? The necklace and a pair of silver ankle bracelets go *chan-chan-chan* as if they were singing.

Dolly flings a few boxes of bangles around in the effort to find matching ones.

Maddie says, "That looks like Christmas," which makes Dolly smile. That's good, Dini thinks. Dolly smiling is better than Dolly distraught and dismayed.

Putting away is almost as surreal. It takes a while, for one thing. It isn't only that Dolly has a whole suitcase full of jewelry and another full of scarves and another full of shoes and so on. It's more that Dolly can't seem to actually *put* anything away. She can take out, model, comment on, and share just fine.

And she can tell stories. The one about the Christmasy necklace sweeps Dini and Maddie away. It's about rich and poor, wrong and right, and Dolly, naturally. Dolly opening her heart and her purse, refusing to let the rich guy cheat the poor one, being strong, fixing everything. Making the good guy feel good and the bad guy feel ashamed. And, naturally, dancing along with her adoring fans.

"Yes!" Dini and Maddie say together. Dolly in real life is like Dolly in the fillums, brave and kind, and all about fairness. What's a little thank-you here and there compared with that?

It would be wonderful if Dolly could be happy as well, but after telling this moving story, she sighs a deep sigh. As the girls put everything away in the silently gliding drawers and the sliding-door cabinets, Dolly returns to being despairing and dejected.

Dad announces, "Time to pack it up, girls. Let's hit the trail."

"Why? No!" Dini has naturally assumed that she and Maddie can stay at this hotel—not forever, of course, but for now. She tries begging. "Just tonight? Why not? Oh please!"

"We can help out!" Maddie chimes in. "We're superefficient."

"We can sleep in the other room. We'll be really quiet."

It is no use.

"Nope," says Dad. "Saddle up, Dini. Back to the ranch."

That night, back at Maddie's, Dini's eyes will not stay shut. Her mind will not clear itself of all the thoughts juggling and jostling for room. Oh, she thought she'd beaten this jet lag thing. Will it ever go away? She thinks maybe she will never sleep again. She imagines herself getting more and more tired from not sleeping, until she is just a lump, unable to move or think or do anything at all. And then how is she going to track down elephants and passports and stuff?

Chapter Eighteen

A Few Questions

OLLIE ONLY MEANT TO ASK A FEW QUEStions. He was curious about the missing passport belonging to the famous movie star, so he did a little searching on the Internet. What he found nearly made him splutter his tea up all over the keyboard.

Someone's selling Dolly's passport on some kind of movie website! It looks like they're auctioning it. There are way too many ads and pop-ups on the page, not to mention some language Ollie can't read, all mixed up with English text. He soon quits in bewilderment. He puts a question out on Twitter, where he sometimes follows topics like *Marathon Chef* and *Dueling Toasters*. He asks:

Fromageur Ollie @Fromageur 20m
Is Dolly Singh famous? #Bollyinfo

A simple yes or no would be enough, but that is not to be. An answer appears soon after.

> **LuvDolly** @finefan 14m
> @Fromageur are you crazy? She's the famousest. Why? #Bollyinfo

Ollie replies:

> **Fromageur Ollie** @Fromageur 12m
> Just asking, @finefan. So if you sold her stuff online, it could be pricey? #Bollyinfo

That really makes them go ape. Ollie wants to duck under the volley of responses.

> **FilmiKumpnee** @fan2fan 9m
> Jewels? Clothes? Selling? Buying? Big auction planned. #Bollyinfo

> **Starstruck** @overthemoon 8m
> Dolly swag? I have green beads if you want to trade. #Bollyinfo

> **FilmiKumpnee** @fan2fan 6m
> Buying/selling Dolly items see filmikumpnee.com.in for updates on this story. #Bollyinfo

Then they begin shooting questions at him, like this one:

> **LuvDolly** @finefan 5m
> What do you have, @Fromageur? How much? #Bollyinfo

And dozens more, demanding to know what he's selling, promising him the moon if he sells his Dolly Singh swag. They are a tide, sweeping Ollie away. See him gulp at his computer screen. He tweets back, "No!" and "Just asking" and "Okay, it's her passport, but I don't have it." This is how rumors begin. Now they all think he's fencing stolen property.

For one minute he wishes he *had* found the passport. *He* could have sold it on the Internet. He could have made enough money to go back to culinary school, to do that extra year specializing in cheese. Then he could go work for that cheese buyer he longs to apprentice with.

The buyer has promised to teach Ollie everything he knows before he retires. After that Ollie could take on running the elderly cheese genius's business. In time it could become his. The Ollie and Alana Cheese Wheel? It's such a vivid daydream it makes his mouth water. But then he tells himself it's all folly. Nonsense. The truth is, he is ashamed of himself for entertaining, even for a minute, the idea of stolen swag.

Chapter Nineteen

Elephant-Proof

SITTING DOWN IS NOT A DRAMATIC ACT. People sit all the time, to a meal, or to work at a desk. If they're young, they sit in school, whether or not they want to. They sit on buses, and if they're lucky enough to find a seat, they sit in trains along the many-colored lines of the Washington, D.C., Metrorail system. They sit because they've been on their feet all day and need a break.

There are hundreds of reasons why a person might sit down. Not one of them is as devastating as the reason the elephant keeper at the National Zoo, Kris Vincenti, sits down on a stone ledge on this beautiful spring day.

One of her elephants is missing.

The door to the yard, which should have been locked at night, is ajar. The rest of the herd huddles inside, where they are supposed to be. But Mini—

that clever and devious young pachyderm—is not there.

Kris gets up from the ledge and runs out into the yard, looking for evidence. In the dirt are the rounded prints of a young elephant tracing a meandering route around the yard and behind a pile of rocks. I counted the elephants at the end of the day, Kris thinks in a panic. How on earth did she get out? And what's this? She picks up a paper bag. An empty lunch bag. She peers at the peanut shell within. She calls her supervisor to break the bad news.

He groans. "Did you check the doors?"

"Of course I did," Kris says. "Before I left. They were fine."

Unspoken visions of the headlines to come float in silence over the phone connection.

"I'll have to inform the city," her boss says.

"Oh, no! You don't want the police after her." With sirens and flashing lights. Kris's heart turns over at the thought.

"Well," he says, "I'll bet you one elephant to twenty golden lion tamarins that within the hour every panicky citizen in the District will be calling Animal Control!"

Kris swallows. He's right. People are not used to friendly young elephants rampaging around in their neighborhoods, even if they are only rampaging gently like Mini.

"Look," she says. "She's not a raccoon in a Dumpster or a squirrel stuck in a chimney. How will they know what to *do* when they find her?"

He sighs. "What do you propose? You know I'm going to call Emergency Services right away. I have to. We have to think about the people of this city."

Kris does not want to think about any people. She is thinking of poor, darling Mini, alone and hungry in the urban wilderness. "I'm going out to look for her," she says, and hangs up.

From the hook on her office wall she grabs the keys to the zoo's truck. She'll need to hitch the trailer on, the special one designed to transport large mammals. As she closes the door behind her, her computer utters a friendly *ping,* announcing incoming e-mail messages, a ping that Kris does not hear.

Chapter Twenty

Tied into Knots

MEANWHILE, FAR AWAY IN THE CITY OF Mumbai, which all the filmi people prefer to call Bombay, in the offices of the famous Starlite Studios, Mr. Soli Dustup (manager, owner, artistic director) is tying himself into knots. Not literally, of course. His delicate constitution could not stand such acrobatics. No, it's his sensitive soul that is twisting and contorting in this way.

Soli has a phone call to return, and he is not looking forward to it. How many times already has he reached for the landline receiver, only to pull back in distress? More times than he can count, and it is only nine in the morning.

"Soli, darling, please ring me at once," says the message, in that voice adored by millions. It sounds a bit quivery. "At once, okay? It's urgent. I don't know how, but someone—well, I don't know if that's true. On the way from the airport—it must have happened on the way from the airport. Or maybe at the airport. Hai, Soli, I'm so afraid, you know, about the opening and all, so I wanted to let you know. Oh, gussa nahin karo, Soli! I've lost—"

Why is she wasting valuable time begging him not to be angry? Now, due to her habit of talking in vaguely trailing sentences, she has run out of time, so her message has been cut off.

It is a classic Dolly cliff-hanger moment.

Urgent? Afraid? Why could she not come to the point? He should call her at once.

And yet, and yet . . . Soli Dustup has been in the movie business long enough that he has developed a pretty reliable mental trouble-meter. He has learned to respect the sensors of this trouble-meter, and right now they are shrieking at high alert. He has a nasty feeling that if he returns that phone call, his present peaceful existence, full of creative projects, artistic endeavors, and lots of rupees from box-office sales, is going to be rudely disrupted.

Much as he adores Dolly, Soli knows that she can scramble, tangle, disrupt, and disarray like nobody else. Her scrambling-tangling talents are quite on par with her superb acting.

He pops a couple of antacids from the sizable jar on his desk and chews them moodily as he speed-dials Dolly's number. "Dolly, darling?" he says in as calming a voice as he can muster.

A flood of words comes pouring into his ear. Soli reels. Autographs, and suitcases. Fans—ceiling or the adoring kind? He can't tell. Some sort of carpet, and Customs officials.

"Soli, are you there?" Dolly says, her voice rising to a glass-shattering pitch. Soli shifts the phone away from his ear while tipping out more digestive pills. He ends up spilling the lot all over his desk.

"No, no, Dolly, love, I wasn't cursing at you," he has to explain. "You lost what? I can't hear you properly. You're in trouble? Customs? You haven't broken any laws?"

The line goes dead.

Soli can feel his insides churning in a most unpleasant manner. He has heard that Americans do not take kindly to people coming from here and there and breaking their laws, and who can blame them?

He shouldn't have let her go on this jaunt. He thought Chickoo could keep an eye on her, but Dolly can make trouble the way other people make cups of tea. Last time Soli let her out of his sight, she threw a diamond ring down a mountainside, nearly wrecking her movie career.

Where is she? Is she not at the Promenade Hotel, where she is supposed to be? He should have asked, "Where are you? What did you lose and why is that against the law?" He toys with the newspaper lying on his desk. It flops open to the World News page. The headline causes him to teeter on his size-eleven feet. It reads: VISA VIOLATORS JAILED IN AMERICA.

Visa trouble? Could it be? Anything's possible with Dolly. The article goes on to say that these visa violators are treated well, given a healthy diet and medical care as needed.

Soli gives vent to a desperate moan. The room appears to heave violently around him like an airplane buffeted by turbulence. Is there anyone he can ask for help? Anyone who is there in America, on the scene, so to speak? That girl—what was her name? Dina? Tina? Dini, that was it. She's there, is she not? He shakes his head. He can't expect a child—even a bright girl who knows a lot about fillums—to bail him out.

Bail. The word makes him quail. What will the gossip magazines make of this? He rings for his assistant. There is no choice. "Book me a flight," Soli says, wincing. "To Washington, D.C. And check my papers, yaar. Make sure the visa is still valid." Governments are fussy about such things.

He braces himself. A long plane trip to America, with Dolly at the other end of it, healthy diet or not—alack and alas, Mr. Soli Dustup does not see soothing effects in sight anytime soon.

Chapter Twenty-One

Not the Same

DINI AWAKES WITH A START, SO SHE MUST have slept after all. The aggravation and disappointment of the day before have not disappeared, exactly, but Dini has things to do. She begins the day in a mad rush so she can get to work.

That is to say, she puts-stuff-away-calls-Dad-has-breakfast-brushes-teeth-makes-her-bed (sort of, and maybe not in that order, but never mind). Then she gets to work.

Maddie looks over Dini's shoulder as she opens up her green-and-silver stripy notebook. It's like old times. Almost. An "Important Grand Opening List" begins to dance onto the page.

Volunteers:

Maddie

Dad

Who else? Chickoo Uncle?

"Put my mom down," Maddie says.

Dini adds her:

Gretchen (Maddie's mom)
Flowers
Dance steps
Rosewater thingies

"What are rosewater thingies?" Maddie wants to know.

"They're stunning." Dini tells her how Dolly was invited to cut a ribbon at the opening of the new wing of Mom's clinic. She gave Dini a little silver container with rose water in it. Dini got to shake it around so all the guests got splashed with the tiny fragrant drops.

"I could do that," Maddie says. "Where do we get one of those?"

"Dolly's got them. And a couple of big brass lamps. You can't have openings and things without them." Dini's glad she got to live in India for ten months and saw an actual opening so she can contribute essential details like this. A clinic is not the same as

a film festival, but an opening is an opening, isn't it? She carries on writing.

> Did the police find anything?
>
> Cake
>
> Props?
>
> Clues?
>
> Cake?

"You wrote 'cake' twice," Maddie points out. "Why the question mark?"

Dini erases the second "cake," leaving streaky marks on the page. She did not mean to write that question mark. There can be no question about the cake. "Maddie," she says, "that chef could make chocolate cake with rose petals, don't you think?"

"Sure?" says Maddie. "Hey, Dini . . ."

"What?"

"Nothing," Maddie says.

If Dini's dad were here, he might point out that there is an elephant in the room. Not a real one, alas, but the kind of metaphorical elephant that people do not want to talk about.

Now Maddie is humming a Dolly song and looking at Dini's list as if there's something elephantine that she wants to say.

"What?" says Dini.

All in a rush Maddie says, "It's just . . . just, you know, that my friend Brenna could help out. She could, really. She'd be great and she's really fun. What do you think?" She waits, as if there is a correct answer and she expects Dini to give it right now.

Oh. Brenna. The new friend Maddie made after Dini went away. "Um," says Dini.

"I told her all about you," Maddie says.

Upon reflection, Dini didn't really want to say "Um." It's an iffy thing to say. She didn't mean to sound iffy. "Um" was not the correct answer. "Sure," she says now, trying to make up.

This whole leaving-and-coming-back business is more complicated than Dini ever imagined. You leave a place, and when you come back, things have changed. A lot can change in ten months. Take Maddie. She is taller. She has braces. She has a new friend.

And Dini? Dini is also taller, true. But how else has she changed? Has she changed at all? She can't tell. She's been running so fast she's meeting herself and she can't tell old and new selves apart.

"Brenna would luuuurve to meet you," Maddie says. "I've told her all about you. She'll come over sometime, maybe during spring break—well, just put her down, okay?"

Dini does.

Brenna (Maddie's friend)

Nothing wrong with that. Maddie can have lots of friends. Look how many friends Dini made in Swapnagiri. But still, it looks funny on the page.

Chapter Twenty-Two

No Elephants

MR. BAYAN, PROGRAM DIRECTOR OF EDUcational and cultural events at the Smithsonian Institution, is a busy man. It is early on Wednesday morning, and the catering problem has not yet been solved. Still, he tries to be polite to the meek, halting voice on the other end of his phone.

"Yes, yes, Mr. Dev," he says. "We're looking forward to the event. I trust you had a pleasant trip."

Something about a passport. Lost, but they're working on getting a replacement. The director makes what he hopes are sympathetic noises.

The man repeats the request.

There is a brief silence, the kind that precedes an explosion—or a dance—in Dolly's fillums. Then, "No," says Mr. B. firmly. "A parade was not in the plan. We were told an opening dance, by a children's group, which is fine."

The voice on the other end persists. Something about a—what? "Excuse me?" he says, although he heard it quite well the first time.

Mr. B. has to swallow his annoyance. He tries to be diplomatic. He tries to remember he is on the staff of a major museum. He is no longer in the United States Marines. But it's hard for him when people insist on making ridiculous requests.

"We'll have a great reception," he assures the nervous man, the fiancé of this Bollywood star whom they will shortly be hosting. "Music. Dancing. The works." He hesitates, then adds, "Refreshments. It'll be grand, don't worry. But no. You must understand. No elephant."

There will be refreshments. Of course. He's working on that problem. He'll solve it. Of course he will. But an elephant? He shakes his head. What next?

Chapter Twenty-Three

Avoiding Inconvenience

TWO TEDIOUS DAYS HAVE GONE BY SINCE Dini's bout of iffiness. Maddie has been in school. Dolly has filled out forms to get a new passport. Dini has gone from iffy to fretful. Dad's done his best to help, but his idea of fun is taking Dini to computer stores. Then, on Wednesday, Dad drops Dini, Dolly, and Chickoo Uncle off at the door of the Consular Wing of the Embassy of India in Washington, D.C., where two friendly stone elephants guard the entrance.

"You go in," Dad says. "I'll find a parking space. It will be like looking for—"

"A needle," Dini says sympathetically.

"In a haystack," he agrees. They both know that needle. Dolly was a needle in a haystack once, when Dini was looking for her.

"You'd better go," Dini says as a police car cruises by.

Dad nods, eases off into the traffic, and is gone.

Passport Section/Consular Wing
Embassy of India, Washington, D.C.
Limited hours
Applications: 9:30 a.m. to 12:30 p.m. weekdays
Pickup: 4:30 p.m. to 5:30 p.m. weekdays
(Please check embassy holiday list.)

To avoid inconvenience,
applicants are requested
to approach the Consular Wing
with a completed application
and all necessary
supporting documents.

Due to restrictions of space and the limited viewpoint available to the person behind the window, the passport section of the Consular Wing of the Indian embassy is not what you might call a hot spot of fun and frolic. "May I help you?" The voice of the person at the window indicates that her day has been full of tedium and she doesn't seriously expect it to get better.

It must be tough, Dini thinks, to sit for half a

day, every day, at a two-foot-by-two-foot window. After a while you might start to think of the whole world as a small square framed in wood. She settles herself into a straight-backed chair next to Dolly's.

"Passport and cake and what else do the fates have in store for me?" says Dolly. "The Smithsonian told Chickoo they've catered the refreshments, but they can't do the cake."

"Don't worry," says Dini. "I think we found someone who can." She tells Dolly about the chef who is due back soon and how Dini's going to talk to him the first chance she gets.

"With rose petal decorations?" says Dolly, surprised.

Dini hesitates for a minute. She thinks of Ollie and Alana worrying what the chef's going to say about Dolly's rose petal milk shakes. But then she thinks, How could even the meanest chef say no to a star? So she nods as surely as she knows how. She nods like she really means it.

"Such a relief," says Dolly, trying to lean back, and failing. "Thank you. That's one worry off my mind!" She sighs. "But for every worry that goes, there are a dozen more. No parade, no elephant. So depressing and dismaying." She manages to cross her legs elegantly even in this uncomfortable chair. Dini wishes she could be half as elegant. The thought just makes her slump.

Chapter Twenty-Four

Temporary Papers

IT IS TOUGH BEING A KID IN A WORLD RUN by people who are not kids. Dini has spent the last ten months in India getting over missing Maddie, so she planned to spend the entire trip to America making up for that.

But their calendars are out of sync. Maddie still has a few days of school before spring break. Dini's school in India is closed this week, and she's taken a few extra days off next week (and will owe them some homework). All for Dolly's sake. She reminds herself to breathe.

On Dolly's behalf, Chickoo Uncle inquires about the status of Dolly's passport application.

"I am trying to explain, sir, but you're not listening," the person at the window says. "We need the old passport along with your completed application for renewal or replacement in order to issue you a new one. Has it been renewed once already? If it has, we can replace. Otherwise we'll simply renew." She waits expectantly, as if she has explained it all and she cannot see why this is not crystal clear to the densest applicant.

"But the old passport is lost!" Chickoo Uncle protests.

"You didn't say that," the person points out. There is a pause. Maybe the window person doesn't like pauses, because she fills it up at once with a volley of words: "Paperwork." "Temporary." "Signature." "Six working days."

Chickoo Uncle droops.

Dolly stirs, fans herself with the end of her scarf. "Chickoo," she calls out, "sab theek-thaak hai?"

This is the same simple question that Dolly's character asks in KHSV: "Is everything all right?" The question galvanizes the leading man into action. So Chickoo at this point should really leap up onto a chair, strike a pose, and break into song: "Kasme tootay, vaadey tootay, mera dil bhi toota!"

But Chickoo Uncle is showing no signs of singing about broken promises causing his heart to break. What is wrong with him? Why doesn't he do something?

Dini catches sight of the digital clock above the window. It is 12:20 p.m. "Oh no!" she cries. "They're going to close in ten minutes."

A ticking clock, as any fillum fan knows, can speed up the most leisurely dance number. Dolly leaps into the fray. She approaches that window. No completed application or supporting documents in hand, but oh wow, does Dolly approach that window! She raises herself to her full height, which isn't much, but somehow she manages to fill the room.

"How did it get lost?" the woman is asking.

"I don't know and I don't care!" Dolly says, pumping her voice up with each word. She leans right into the window, never mind that she has to stand on tiptoe to do so. "Tell me where to sign." Such a storm of beads and rings flings loose that the window person steps back in a hurry.

"Twelve twenty-two," whispers Dini, right at Dolly's elbow.

The window person stares. "I know you," she says, tottering where she stands.

And suddenly it's as if music fills the air. As if trees loaded with bottlebrush flowers unfurl their branches in the stucco-ceilinged room and dip in a little bow to the clock and the window and the picture of Mahatma Gandhi on the wall. As if the chairs might get up and do a little dance all by themselves.

"Dolly Singh?" the window lady whispers. And stares. Gulps. And stares.

Dolly smiles serenely. "Yes."

"Twelve twenty-four," says Dini.

The window lady gets her voice back. What a recovery. And now suddenly she moves at lightning speed. She whips out forms and pens, and makes little *x*'s in all the places where Dolly needs to sign. Dolly Singh? Vah! Of course she'll get her an emergency certificate, for ID purposes. "Use it here. Travel home. No problem. Is it true that you're going to be releasing a fillum here in Washington? Dolly? Really? Array vah!"

Dolly chats happily, signing away as if she were autographing for a fan, which maybe she is.

Chickoo Uncle runs his finger around the inside of his shirt collar in weary relief.

Soon Dolly has completed her form. Her picture has been stuck to the paper, and it's been signed by all the right people. The woman keeps a copy and gives Dolly one. They will let her use that instead of her passport to travel back to India.

"What about the lost passport?" Dini asks.

"It will be documented in the system as lost," says the woman.

"What a relief!" Dolly says. "Then it's all right."

She says it as if that will take care of it. But isn't the lost passport still out there somewhere? No one appears to be worrying about that. Maybe, Dini thinks, I don't need to worry either. All is well, fine, and complete. Like a dance that begins at center stage and spirals out and out until the end, when the center draws everyone back in again, and the lights go down. . . .

And Dini? Right at this moment she is experiencing the odd sensation of being a little—well, unnecessary. Dolly, after all, is managing fine. The clock has ticked itself right out of time and no one is paying attention to it. The window woman is bringing her colleagues to meet Dolly, who is inviting them all to the opening.

Dolly catches Dini's eye and blows her a friendly kiss. She says, "And my dearest young fans, Dini and her friend Gladdie, will put on a grand opening dance. Isn't that wonderful?"

The entire embassy staff is now staring at Dini. Someone is bringing cups of tea. Someone else is offering trays of crunchy snacks, all in honor of Dolly.

"Maddie," Dini says to no one in particular, which is just as well because no one is listening. "Her name's Maddie."

Chapter Twenty-Five

Chef!

OLLIE, LINE COOK AT THE PROMENADE HOtel's Urban Delight Restaurant, is whispering to Alana, the sous-chef, over lunch prep. "There's all kinds of stuff on Twitter about her."

"Who?"

"Dolly. The Bollywood star. You know. Dolly Singh." He jerks his chin at the hotel suites in the floors above their small kitchen universe.

"Dolly, huh?" she says. "What are they saying about her?"

"Stuff," says Ollie mysteriously. "She's famous. Imagine."

"Imagine," says Alana, and her face is terribly close to his and her eyes sparkle in a way that threatens to dislocate his vocal cords.

"WHAT'S going on in my KITCHEN?" The sudden roar makes Alana and Ollie leap back from their cozy chat. Now Ollie's elbow, hitting a shelf, is in danger of dislocation.

In culinary circles it is well known that Chef Armend Latifi's anger can make brave souls cower. Alana and Ollie cower now. Cowering is the sensible thing to do.

The chef lifts random lids, opens bags in the refrigerator. He checks suspiciously in each container, each bag. He peers under the counters as if expecting to surprise burglars. What a comedown this is, his frown suggests. Just days ago he was hobnobbing with culinary geniuses at international conventions. Now he has to face a couple of soulless ignoramuses who don't know a Berliner from a Boston cream pie. "RoseroseROSE petals?" he roars.

Alana looks at Ollie. Ollie looks at Alana.

"Rose petals?" the chef demands. "Whatwhatwhat are you playing at?"

A nervous laugh comes bubbling up inside Ollie. He gulps it back down.

"She requested it specially," Alana says, startling Ollie into a spasm.

Chef Armend wheels around. "Requested, eh?" he sneers. "Well, let me tell you. I, Armend Latifi, do not take requests. The menu is MY daily masterpiece! Do you understand?" His fist crashes down onto the counter.

Ollie flinches. He does not mean to. Flinching is ruinous to his state of mind, especially with Alana looking.

"DoyoudoyouDOyou?" demands Chef Armend, brandishing the bag of rose petals.

"Yes, Chef," Ollie mutters, trying to look away. The shaking bag makes him dizzy.

"It was a special order, Chef." Alana is so brave, trying to spread reason. "From the guest in five oh three, Dolly Singh. She's fond of rose petal milk shakes. We tried a few variations."

Oh, that Alana! Ollie realizes he has admired her for as long as he's worked in this restaurant. She is just so . . . admirable! A kind of warrior type, filled with fierce loyalty and . . . and—oh, it's an old-fashioned word, but honor! Alana has honor in spades. Ollie regrets greatly that he is not the honorable warrior type himself.

She's going on. She won't give up. Oh, she is relentless. "With a little honey—she liked that one a lot, the kids said. Or with a dash of . . ."

But here at last Alana's voice wavers, making Ollie's heart whirl around inside him like a blender on the highest setting.

"Cayenne pepper!" He doesn't mean to blurt it out. Alana's voice is doing that to him, making him take risks he never intended to take.

"No!" the chef yells. "NO! Awayawayaway!"

Oh, now Ollie's done it. Is the chef firing Alana? It's all my fault, Ollie thinks miserably.

Alana takes off her sous-chef's hat with a sigh. "Okay, Chef."

"Wait a minute," says Ollie's voice, once again saying things that he himself would never dare to utter. "Fine. Me too. I'm leaving with her."

The line cook Ollie replaced had warned him. "Watch out," he'd said. "This guy fires assistants like a BB gun fires pellets."

But the chef has stopped short. "Stopstopstop! *Where* are you off to?"

He is not ordering them out after all. "Oh, tragedy and sorrows!" It's the bag of rose petals he's talking to. "I cannot bear the sight!" he bellows. His face twists in agony. Alana hands the bag to Ollie. "Put it away," she whispers.

Rose
PICKED: 4/1

Ollie spirits the bag to the very back of the refrigerator.

"Now then," says the chef, collecting himself with an effort. "Room five oh three, you say?"

They nod in silence.

"I'll explain, that's it, explain," he mutters. "She must, she has to; of course she'll see reason. Rose petals—aaah! Out of the question." He is speaking to the utensils hanging from their hooks now, or to the ceiling.

Armend Latifi's is a secret sorrow. His family came to America from a country named Albania. When he was but a child, his grandmother used to take him for walks to the botanical garden right here in Washington, D.C. Her favorite flowers were the roses.

Sadly, Armend's beloved Nona died the very year that he graduated with his culinary arts diploma. He himself planted a rosebush on her grave to mark the occasion.

She never lived to see his success, his accomplishments, his stellar ratings in restaurant reviews. And so the mere mention of roses is a terrible reminder to him. Just say the word, and the chef becomes, as

Dini's dad might say, "as crazy as popcorn on a hot skillet."

Now Armend Latifi shudders from head to toe. He straightens his toque and walks out, a lonely soldier against the forces seeking to assault his kitchen and his peace of mind.

"Thanks, Ollie," Alana says in a small voice.

"You're welcome." Her eyes are melting him the way a hot skillet melts a pat of butter. "*I* thought you were wonderful."

"You did?"

"You were—I did—you were magnificent." There. It is said. He does think so. She is.

"Oh, Ollie," says Alana.

"Oh, Alana," says Ollie.

A scene like this one is worthy of being in one of Dolly's epic fillums. Such tension! Such drama. There should be music. Ollie and Alana should sing. They might find a tree and dance around it. But since this is reality and not the movies, the best they can do is to go on repeating themselves.

Chapter Twenty-Six

Help Out by Watching Out

DAD PULLS UP TO THE CURB, STOPS, TURNS his flashers on. He honks at Dini & Co., a suggestion to hurry up.

Dolly is not taking suggestions. "Dini!" she calls. It's a final photo op, Dolly with the consulate staff on the steps, between those friendly stone elephants. Elephants! Dini should be in that picture.

Dad gets out of the car. The driver of an articulated Metrobus, one of those double buses joined together accordion-style in the middle, honks at Dad for messing up the nicely flowing traffic. Dad comes running around a statue of Gandhi, urging his uncooperative passengers to get in the car fast before he is slapped with a ticket.

Dini would love-love-love to be in that picture, but the camera's clicking already.

Too late. She tells herself it doesn't matter. The

photo isn't so important right now. Because the ad on the side of that articulated Metrobus has caught her attention. Caught it and held it and shown her how she matters. The ad says: HELP OUT BY WATCHING OUT! It's supposed to be about national security, but really, Dolly requires the same kind of thinking.

So simple. So brilliant. Helping out by watching out is what a good and true fan does.

As the photo op ends and they all pile into the car, Dini decides not to articulate her ideas. She can see the importance of them, but Dad will say she's just being nosy.

She gets a chance to put her new motto into action sooner than she expects, because a few blocks down Embassy Row, Dolly declares that she needs to buy some stamps. "I have some fan letters I must reply to," she says. "Maybe we can find some pretty stamps."

"Nick of time," Dad says, and pulls into a side street. "Here's the post office. Hmm, question is, can I find parking anywhere?"

"Dad," Dini says, "let me go get the stamps. You just keep driving around."

"That's my girl," says Dad. "Dini to the rescue."

"Airmail stamps," Dolly says. "Ten, in nice colors. Thank you, Dini, darling."

"Don't forget to come back for me," Dini says, grabbing the money from Chickoo Uncle.

She dashes into the post office, stands in line. The clerk wants to palm off plain old stamps with airplanes, but "I need a nicer picture," Dini says.

Grumbling, the clerk pulls out a sheet with rocks and marsh grass on it. "That's a national park. Will that do you?"

The stamps have a French-looking word on them. "Where is that?" says Dini.

"That'll be eight dollars," the woman replies. She is uninterested in small talk.

On her way out Dini stops short. Look at that poster! It has a picture of her stamp. It's a national park in Minnesota, named Voyageurs. Dini is not sure how to say that, and she has never been to Minnesota. She has been all the way to India and back, but not to Minnesota. She should go someday.

Tapping her feet and humming "haan-haan-haan," she waits outside the post office for Dad to drive up. There he is! Dini climbs back in the car.

Dolly promptly declares that she adores the

stamps. "I love nature," she says. "The rocks are gold, not silver, but still, quite idyllic and perfect, I must say. Hai na, Chickoo?"

Chickoo Uncle agrees with Dolly. Dad agrees with Chickoo Uncle. Dini has to admit that Dolly, in her jeweled finery, is not exactly the outdoor type. In fact, in real life Dolly would probably not recognize nature if it showed up and bit her on the foot. Still, she can put up a fine show of being outdoorsy in the fillums. And all this agreeing is . . . quite agreeable.

Before Dini can say anything, Dad turns right onto Connecticut Avenue, causing four jaws to drop simultaneously.

This is not on account of his faulty driving. He did not run over a pothole and cause any dislocation of joints. No, it is shock. This normally peaceful artery, along which traffic runs in smooth and regulated fashion, has been transformed into a scene that could rival the one in KHSV where the big chase has ended and the villain has been cornered. Where no one in the crowd knows if it's all over, or if there's one last round of drama, song, and dance. In other words, total chaos.

Chapter Twenty-Seven

Finding a Mark

ALONG THE SPACIOUS AVENUES AND ON THE sidewalks of the city, Mini is causing a stir.

"Where'd it go?"

"That way!"

"No, this way!"

"Did you see that? An elephant! It was ripping leaves off the trees on Kalorama Road!"

"Now it's back on Connecticut Avenue!"

People in roaring machines have been following Mini, talking to one another on small, crackly boxes. They are coming closer and closer.

All she wants is something to eat. She has found herself going around and around in a circle, but no one will stop for her. There are plenty of people walking along, but they are not inclined to share their lunches. Instead, upon seeing her, they scream and run in all directions.

"Eek!"

"Watch out!"

"Hey, traffic goes that way, heffalump!"

Mini steps and steps and runs and trots, all kinds of moving she's never had much of a chance to do before. Now the sky is filling with the sounds of wings, but they are not bird wings, some other kind of machine wings that go around and around. All this circling is making poor Mini dizzy. And the people-talk. So much people-talk.

"Run! Run!"

"Hey! Look at that!"

"You think it's dangerous?"

"Outta my way!"

Perhaps the memory of her little yard at the zoo is beginning to call to Mini with longing and some regret.

"Maybe they're making a movie!"

"Get a picture, quick!"

"They'll never believe this back home in Charmington!"

"Call the fire department!"

"9-1-1? An elephant! South of Dupont Circle. You know already? DO something!"

High above the fray, in a fire truck, a walkie-talkie crackles. A firefighter is being paged by his supervisor. "It's running down Connecticut again, sir," he says. "Boy, it's pretty quick. I didn't think elephants could run like that. Yeah, toward the post office! We're on it. Over."

Crackle, crackle.

"Yeah," he says, "we got a fella from Animal Control with us. Yup, he's got a dart gun. Over and out."

"I'm not so sure about the dosage," says the Animal Control man. "I've never done an elephant before, know what I mean?"

The firefighters in the truck laugh and crack jokes. "Dangerous animal, bud," says one, grinning at the Animal Control man, who blanches. "Sure you can handle this?"

The team leader calls, "All right, let's hit the ground!" They scramble out of the truck.

On the ground the drama intensifies.

"Mama, elephant!" says a toddler, enchanted. His mother scoops him up, turns to head home.

"Mama, wanna elephant!" The child wriggles.

"Come on, angel, let's get outta here."

"ELEPHANT! Wanna ELEPHANT!"

❀ ❀ ❀

Poor baby. Kris has been driving the zoo truck all over northwest D.C. and she's closing in. She can see the fire truck now, sirens blaring, with police cars close behind. Overhead the medical emergency helicopters circle. Has Mini—oh, terrible thought!—hurt someone?

Heart in mouth, she screeches to a halt, scrambles out of the van. She runs toward the crowd, the trucks, the police cars with their rotating, flashing blue-red-blue lights.

Kris is not generally a praying kind of person, but she now finds herself appealing to someone on high, anyone faintly God-ish, to protect her sweet Mini. And the people, too, yes, people who don't know any better, who might panic and do something to . . .

Oh no! Who's that? She sees the firefighters, and she sees a man in a different kind of uniform. She catches her breath. What is he holding in his hand? A dart gun? No, no, no!

Several things then happen at once, as if they have been choreographed, complete with sound effects.

A child wriggles down from his mother's arms.

He breaks free, runs. "ELEPHANT!" he squeals.

The mother screams.

Mini rears up onto her hind legs. She trumpets in alarm, a clear, panicked shriek that ricochets off the buildings lining the road.

The firefighters surge forward. The Animal Control man raises his dart gun.

"Mini!" Kris cries. "Mini, sweetheart. It's me!" She throws herself between the dart gun and her precious pachyderm, yelling, "No! Don't shoot! Just let me talk to her!"

Click! Whiz! The dart flies through the air. It misses Kris by inches. It misses Mini, too.

But it finds a mark in someone's arm—a mild-mannered man with untidy hair who has just made his entrance. He has, alas, taken the hit before he can dance a single step. With a sigh he now collapses in a heap.

"Rats!" yells the Animal Control man.

Chapter Twenty-Eight

Chickoo!

"LOOK!" DINI CRIES AS DAD BRAKES AND brakes again, sliding to a stop at the police barrier across Connecticut Avenue. "An elephant!" She has been worrying about providing Dolly with an elephant. Who knew that one would show up like magic, right on the streets of D.C.?

"Where?" says Dolly. "Oh, I've been longing for an elephant! I adore them."

Dini points. The elephant has disrupted traffic, causing much honking, shaking of fists, and uttering of colorful words.

"Hai, it's just like *Haathi mere saathi!*" Dolly cries, referring to the old classic fillum in which an elephant rescues a small boy from an attacking leopard and revives him by sprinkling water on his face. The boy becomes an honorary friend of all elephants and the best friend of one in particular.

It's sooo . . . ! No wonder it's one of Dolly's favorite old fillums.

"Such a lovely surprise!" Dolly cries. "An elephant tamasha just for me! Chickoo darling, you didn't tell me!"

She thinks the elephant fun is all for her! Before anyone can point out that it isn't, Dolly flings the car door open, kicks her strappy silver sandals away, and is off. She's running barefoot down Connecticut Avenue, ducking under the yellow tape, aiming for the heart of the scene.

Chickoo Uncle exits next, calling, "Stop! Dolly!"

And now it's Dini's turn.

"Hey!" Dad shouts. "Whoa! Dini! You stay right here."

Too late. Dini has always been a fast runner, and at this moment she outdoes herself. She has to. There's Dolly disappearing into the crowd and Chickoo Uncle after her. Now he's overtaking Dolly, and the elephant's rearing up, and there's screaming and shouting and—

Dini's helping out by watching out, but oh no! What's this?

It's a man with a gun! A gun! Okay, so she was

wrong about the people with guns at the airport, but this is different. Here in the streets of Washington, D.C., a real-life movie of the most alarming kind is playing out. If Dini doesn't do something, then no one will.

Almost there. Her feet are flying. They barely touch the ground. She reaches. Grabs. "Watch out!" she cries as she pulls Dolly down to the sidewalk with her.

Dolly screams, that scream that fans in India

know so well and fans in America are just about to get acquainted with.

But one girl, even a girl who runs fast and makes slidy, dancy moves with light and easy steps, can't do it all, can she? Dini has managed to save Dolly from being hit by the dart that flies out of that gun. But Chickoo Uncle, brave, gallant Chickoo Uncle, has taken the projectile squarely in the shirtsleeve.

With a soft sigh, as if the air has been let out of him unexpectedly, Chickoo crumples to the ground.

Chapter Twenty-Nine

In the Fast Lane

BY THE TIME SOLI DUSTUP ARRIVES AT Thurgood Marshall Airport, also known as Baltimore-Washington International, he is feeling as if he has been knocked down by a bulldozer and dragged across a couple of continents. It was early Wednesday morning in India when he left, and on account of the turning of the Earth, it is still Wednesday here on his arrival. That makes it one long and nauseating Wednesday.

That last patch of turbulence over the ocean had him clenching his teeth so tightly that it's a wonder they are still intact. He is dizzy. His head hurts. Sharp, shooting pains are making themselves felt in his right shoulder. Stormy words are flashing through his mind, words that he will utter to his favorite fillum star when he finds her.

Where to begin looking? That is his worry

right now. To what luxurious jail with recreational programs and healthy food options do they take movie stars who break American laws? And what did she do, anyway, to get herself into this fix?

That Dolly. She's capable of anything. Remember the time she left Bombay and went off to some little place in the mountains, leaving Soli to deal with lashings of unopened mail and masses of disgruntled fans? And what about when she decided to dance her way to the top of the parliament building in Delhi, leaving poor Chickoo to face a squad of security men in riot gear? Oh, Dolly, my love, Soli thinks, you have much to answer for.

With his passport checked and stamped, his papers examined, but his mind still in turmoil, Soli Dustup drags his bags to a curbside bench, plunks himself down, and ponders his next step.

He should take a taxi. But to where? He considers a few possible options. "Take me to the local prison, my man." No, that is not quite it.

"FBI headquarters, please, sir." That has possibilities.

He could produce the photo of Dolly that he has prudently tucked into his suitcase. He could say, "Has this beautiful lady been in the local news lately?"

Oh, it is very difficult to be following the trail of a star like Dolly. She dazzles, but she is also a moving target. A shooting star, he thinks gloomily.

Just then someone taps Soli's shoulder, that same shoulder that has recently been assaulted by vicious stabs of pain. Mr. Dustup leaps aside, nearly falling off the bench. Combine shock with an already traumatized rotator cuff, and you get a leaping studio executive.

When the dust settles around Soli, his shoulder still twinges but he sees that there is no cause for worry. It is only a cabdriver. "Taxi, sir?"

The man looks like a hardworking sort of chap, although not movie material. Needs a shave, and has one tooth missing. Still, Soli himself needs a shave after so many hours on planes, and it is only pure luck that his teeth, fillings and all, are still in his jaw. He nods gratefully.

"Where to, sir?"

"That's a very good question." Mr. Soli Dustup's woes come crashing in on him.

It is not in Soli's nature to bare his troubles to a

total stranger. But given his fragile state of being, what choice does he have? He tells the cabdriver all about Dolly and the grand premiere of KHSV, the phone message, and now his uneasy feeling that she is in some kind of trouble.

"Are you sure, sir?" the driver says. "Dolly Singh?"

"Herself," says Soli.

"In trouble? No, no, no. Far from it. Just look." Settling Soli in the backseat of his cab, the driver hands him a copy of the Entertainment section of the local paper, which is none other than the well-regarded *Washington Post*. Even in far-off Bombay, Mr. Dustup has heard of the *Post*. The driver goes off to load Soli's bags into the trunk of his vehicle.

BOLLYWOOD STAR TO OPEN FESTIVITIES AT SMITHSONIAN'S INDIA SCREENFEST says the lead item. Silently, Soli blesses the cabdriver. The man may not look much like a guardian angel, but impressions can deceive.

As the driver closes the trunk, Soli reads the identification card in the cab. Tariq Hasan. That is the man's name. A good name. Looks like a solid sort of man, to match that reliable-sounding name.

Someone who knows what's what and is up on the news that counts.

Now Soli reads the newspaper article. Of prisons it makes no mention. It assures him that the grand opening of KHSV is on as scheduled. Dolly is to cut a ribbon, make a speech, and grace the red-carpet event with her presence. "I am very excited to be here in this great city to launch your festival," she is quoted as saying. Would she say that if she were languishing in prison, however well fed she might be?

Various distinguished guests are expected to attend, the article goes on, including the ambassador of India herself and some members of Congress. It is a matter-of-fact piece of writing, intended to inform. To Soli it brings a wave of comfort, causing the rotator cuff in his shoulder joint to ease up on his nerve endings.

Perhaps, after all, he read too much into Dolly's phone call. Perhaps, though he is a movie man, he somehow did not see the whole picture.

Tariq Hasan gets behind the wheel, murmuring, "She's a great star. A number one star."

Soli perks up. Fans are his business. "You know Dolly's movies?"

"Of course I do," says the driver, turning the key in the ignition so the engine purrs to life. "I'm from Bangladesh myself. Dhaka."

"We're neighbors!" cries Soli in delight, forgetting the fifteen hundred miles between Dhaka, the capital of Bangladesh, and his own beloved city of Bombay. He tells him all about the legacy he plans to leave to that city—the Bolly-Dazzle Museum, with a permanent exhibit featuring Dolly herself. "Opened just this year. You should visit it sometime. Free entry. Tell them I sent you."

The driver thanks him fervently as he pulls out into traffic. "I will definitely go to your fine museum one day," he says. "My whole family is crazy about Dolly movies. Dolly herself came to Dhaka once on a tour, you know."

"Of course I know," Soli says with pride. "I blinking organized that tour, my friend."

"She sang a song in Bangla, our own beautiful language," says Tariq Hasan. "Oh, the crowds went wild." Greatly moved by the memory he hums a stanza of the song.

"A fan!" Soli marvels. Dolly really is a miracle worker. Where she goes, fans follow.

But his doubts still cast a shadow. "So you don't think she's in jail, then?"

The driver laughs a merry laugh.

"So what was all that she said about doing against-the-law things? Something she lost, she said. Something about Customs officials." Mr. Dustup himself has had a few run-ins with officials in India, one over a small matter of importing studio equipment. The memory still disturbs his sleep.

Tariq Hasan declares that any officials present at Dolly's arrival must have been there to welcome her. "She is a star," he says. "They came to get her autograph. How can she be anywhere but safe and sound in her hotel room? So"—he turns onto a ramp, then eases deftly onto a road where the traffic is shooting past at terrifying speed—"where to, sir?"

"All right, my good man," says Soli, trying not to clutch the seat each time a truck whirs past. "Take me to the Promenade Hotel."

These roads make his stomach lurch. Roads in his beloved Bombay are also jam-packed with traffic and rife with the potential for chaos, but he knows those roads. This traffic is very—

Mr. Dustup flinches as a giant truck thunders by. Much too—

He ducks as the driver speeds up to change lanes.

Fast. This is what they mean when they say that people live life in the fast lane in America. Not that they are slow in Bombay, not a bit of it. But fifty-five miles per hour is too fast.

Chapter Thirty

Remotely Heroic

KRIS HAS NEVER DONE ANYTHING REMOTELY heroic in her life, and she knows in her bones that throwing herself into the void is in that category.

And Mini, sweet Mini. When she hears Kris's voice, she hesitates. Still in midair, she catches Kris's eye. She stops, sways for a minute. Slowly, slowly, she comes back down. Her forelegs touch the ground. Her trunk slumps. She sits. Sits and stays as Kris has taught her to.

Kris runs up to her, hugs the wrinkly head with its blinky eyes and little prickly hairs on the top, strokes the flappy ears. Her eyes mist over from relief, or joy, or both. "It's all right," she says to anyone who needs to know, especially the pushy police and fire people who keep getting in her face. "I'm her keeper. National Zoo, Kris Vincenti.

Look, here's my ID. Yes, I've got a trailer to take her back. It's all right."

The rescue teams disperse the crowds. The ambulance takes away the man who caught the dart in his arm. He is making small whuffly noises, so at least he's alive.

Then Kris leads Mini to the trailer and secures her inside for the ride back to the zoo. She knows she has to do this. It is her job, after all. She has to get Mini back to where she belongs.

Getting into the trailer, Mini turns her head. She flaps an ear at Kris. Her small, bright eyes blink.

Kris melts. Somewhere deep inside, although she knows it is a foolish thought for a professional zookeeper, she knows she's let Mini down.

"You just wanted a little fun," she says. "You didn't mean any harm."

Mini flaps her other ear.

"I'm sorry, baby," Kris says. "I'll make it up to you. I promise." Although as she secures the trailer, then gets in the truck and pulls out onto the road, she has no idea how she's going to do a thing like that.

Chapter Thirty-One

A Wrinkle in the Plotline

THE DAY GOES BY IN A BLUR OF HOW-DID-this-happen and will-he-be-all-right and oh-what-a-terrible-omen-this-is! The local hospital pronounces Chickoo alive, if a little dazed due to the dose of tranquilizer that accidentally found its way into him. "Not enough for an elephant, thank goodness," the doctor says. He raises an eyebrow at Chickoo Uncle. "Just be grateful for Animal Control's incompetence."

Dini tries to avoid meeting Dad's eye, which she is afraid may not be wearing a pleased look. She is right about that. "Dini," Dad says to her, "listen to me." Which is altogether un-Dadly and makes Dini shuffle from foot to foot and feel guilty.

"I know," Dini says. "I know what you're going to say, Dad, but really—"

At this point Dolly intervenes. She says firmly,

"He's going to say shabaash, brava, well done, Dini darling. What else could he say, my dearest friend and fan?"

"Hmm, well . . ." Dad backs off, but the glint in his eye says, Later, Dini, later.

"You saved my life!" Dolly declares.

And Dini thinks, I did? And then she thinks, Well, that may be overstating it a bit. Still, just imagine if *Dolly* had taken that dart in the arm instead of Chickoo Uncle.

Back at the hotel there are three messages waiting for Dini. "Dini, where have you been?" Maddie demands when Dini returns her call. "I called as soon as I got back from school. We were getting worried."

"Wait'll I tell you," says Dini, and she does.

There is a small silence at the other end. Then Maddie says, "Oh. Freaky. He was stunned. Literally."

"Yup," says Dini. "Valium. Did you know that's what they put into elephant darts?"

"No," Maddie says. "Hope you're taking notes, Dini. That's a plotline right there."

"No kidding," says Dini.

Maddie says she thinks it's a twist in the plotline, or no—wait—a wrinkle. "Wrinkle—elephants? Get it?" she says.

"I get it," says Dini. For the first time since she met Dolly, she wonders if she is in over her head. How many story lines can she juggle in her mind, each with its own wrinkles and stumbles? She has a feeling that the wrinkling and stumbling has only just begun.

Chickoo is resting in bed, with Dolly at his side. She holds an ice pack to his head over his feeble protests. Dad is starting to make we-have-to-leave-now noises.

"Meet you downstairs," Dini tells him.

"Where are you going now?" says Dad. Dini does not like the sound of that "now."

"Just to the kitchen," she mutters, and she's off the phone before he can ask why. She is poking her nose into rose petal chocolate cakes, and she doesn't want to be stopped. As she hurries toward the elevator, she practices what she'll say to the surreally grumpy chef.

"Would you consider making a very special cake," she might say, "for a very special occasion?" Or, "I want to talk to you about an international movie opening. We need a cake. But not just any cake." Or, "How do you feel about rose petals?"

Sometimes a person thinks she is saying something in the quiet of her own private mind, when really she has spoken the thought out loud. This happens to Dolly's character in KHSV, which gives away the fact that she's thrown a valuable diamond ring down the mountainside, leading the crook to scramble down after it and break his arm.

The same thing happens now to Dini. Not the breaking-of-bones part, but thinking out loud. "How do you feel about rose petals?" The elevator door opens just as Dini realizes she is speaking those words aloud. The man in the blinding white uniform hears them.

Ping . . . ping . . . The elevator door tries to close, but he's in the way, frozen. Rose petals . . . rose petals . . . rose petals . . . The words seem to echo in this stalled scene.

Then, "OUT of my way!" roars Chef Armend, stepping forward and nearly knocking Dini off her feet. He races down the hallway.

"Stop!" Dini cries. What is he doing hammering on the door of room 503?

The door opens. The chef's tall white hat twinkles out of sight.

Whoa! He's rushing right back out again! Back toward the elevator, and now Dolly is following him. "How dare you?" she cries, flinging jewelry in all directions. Off they go, zig-zig-zag toward the elevator:

"How dare you complain about my milk shake order

when my dearest darling fiancé

is lying in bed after having

been struck by a dart?

Do you know that?

He was struck by a dart!

Struck down! Lost consciousness!

Imagine my distress, praying for his safe recovery,

and here you are prattling on

about

MILK SHAKES?"

"Can we talk . . . please?" the chef pleads, backing away and raising his arms against the flying missiles. His white hat teeters on the verge of collapse.

What a dance, all the way to the elevator! Such footwork. Such rhythm. Perfect pacing.

The chef hits the elevator button as if his life depends on it. "Rose petals?" he says pitifully. "Why not a pistachio milk shake? Or cranberry orange?" A glittering bracelet whizzes past his head.

Dolly lifts her face. She sets her chin. Who can cross her now? "No," she says. "I must have my rose petal milk shake with chocolate sprinkles. How else can I make it through this extremely stressful trip? How?"

The elevator arrives. The chef bows his head and ducks inside.

Dolly shakes her head briskly. "What an annoying man," she says. "What is his problem?"

From the descending elevator, sounds of distress can be heard. They are the defeated expressions of a strong-willed man who has just met his match.

Chapter Thirty-Two

Only Five Days Left

ON THE WAY TO MADDIE'S, DAD GIVES DINI an earful. He is very clear about his feelings on plotlines, never mind if they're wrinkled or filled with rose petals. No more antics like today's. What if she, Dini, had been jabbed by the dart? So it wasn't enough to kill a grown man, but a twelve-year-old? Dad is upset enough that for the whole twenty minutes to the Maryland state line, he does not use a single Western idiom. He is supposed to be her buddy and vocabulary consultant for the fillums, and here he is going all parental on her.

"You sound like Mom," Dini says as they drive down Piney Branch and into the city of Takoma Park.

"Doing my best," says Dad.

"Me too," says Dini sadly.

Dad sighs. As he turns onto Maddie's street and stops at the house with white painted trim, he says something about real life and movies and how they are not the same thing. Then he says, "Well. Only five days left until the opening, and then we're off." He says it as if it's supposed to make her feel better.

Dini rings the doorbell. Maddie lets her in. Dad waves as he drives away. Dini waves back, but it is a halfhearted wave.

"On the heels of today's incident on Connecticut Avenue," says the newscaster on the bedside radio in Maddie's mom's room, "a faulty lock has been reported to be the cause of the young elephant Mini's escapade. Apparently, the lock is under a manufacturer's recall notice. Upon entering the necessary codes, the lock appears to be secured, yet when sufficient pressure is applied to the door, it yields, making the door easy to push open. In sports news . . ."

"That's how she got out!" Dini says.

"Wish I'd been there," says Maddie. "Stupid braces had to be fixed today." She worries the braces with her tongue, which she's not supposed to do. It makes Dini run her tongue over her own teeth in sympathy.

Chapter Thirty-Three

Better with Three

THE FOLLOWING MORNING MADDIE HAS TO go to school. Gretchen drops her off, and Dini goes along so she can get to see Maddie's new school. It's middle school, since Maddie's now in sixth grade. The building looks big, and it's bursting with kids Dini does not know, so she feels a bit out of sorts, out of scene, and in general out of it. It's no fun.

She's quiet in the car, going back with Maddie's mom, who gives her a couple of curious looks but says nothing. Gretchen will be working at home that day. "Are you going to be okay, hanging out all by yourself?" she asks Dini. "I'll just be in the office room, so let me know if you need anything."

"Okay," says Dini, but really, what can she possibly ask for? Perfect dance steps would be good. Also a cake worthy of a star. Somehow she can't see Maddie's mom coming up with either.

Dini spends lots of time riffling through Maddie's bookshelves and watching Dolly videos, and then some time just sort of staring into the middle distance. As it turns out, the slow pace of the day is almost a relief after the frantic excitement of the day before. At the end of it she's feeling more in control, and her natural optimism is beginning to reassert itself. She thinks, I will pull this dance together, and it will be just fine.

She's just wondering if the opening steps should be really fast or just dramatic and what kind of hand movements signal drama when Maddie's mom comes in. She has segued from her accounting work to laundry, and holds a hamper of clothes that need to be folded.

"Look who just came home," she says.

Maddie's back, and she's brought a visitor.

A tall girl peeks from behind Gretchen, Maddie's laundry-carrying, prop-toting mom.

"Hi," says the tall girl tripping into the room. "I'm Brenna. Ask me why I've been waiting to meet you." She stands on one leg and spins around quickly three times while asking the question.

Dini is wobbly just watching her. Maddie laughs.

Dini does not know what to say, which is a new feeling for her. "Ask me," Brenna persists.

"Why have you been waiting to meet me?" Dini asks, feeling a bit silly. It is what Dad would call a loaded question. What if she doesn't like the answer?

"Tons of reasons," says Brenna enthusiastically, stretching one hand behind her back and catching it with the other, a feat that Dini herself could never pull off. "Because you're Maddie's friend. And because of Dolly. Isn't Dolly, like, a dozen reasons right there, all by herself?" She raises herself up on tiptoe and spins around again.

Dini steps back to get out of the way, and ends up sitting down with a thump on Maddie's bed. "I guess," she says, and finds herself blinking.

Maddie's mom laughs. "You girls," she says fondly, in the manner of one speaking to puppies whose friskiness is getting out of hand. "You're—how do you say it? Stunning?" She picks an escaped sock up off the floor.

"Us?" says Dini, startled.

"Stunning," says Gretchen, plunking the sock back in the basket.

"Mom," says Maddie. "You can't get it right. Don't even try."

"Stun*ning*," Maddie and Brenna say together, with the emphasis on the second syllable.

"I'll leave you all to be stunned together," Maddie's mom says. "Don't forget to fold the laundry."

I can say "stunning," Dini thinks. I can say it right.

But she doesn't.

MERA
JEEVAN
DOLLY SINGH
HI!

Chapter Thirty-Four

Across Many Time Zones

DINI AND MADDIE RUSH THROUGH THE laundry, and Brenna helps too, although half the time she's juggling the clothes. They dance the dance until they collapse in a heap. Brenna catches on fast, and even Maddie's getting over her Egyptian tomb–person instincts.

"We should have something to hold in our hands," Dini says. "You know what I mean? If we put it in the middle and then pick it up when we go in and out, that'll look stunning."

"Okay, but what's this 'it'?" says Maddie.

"Ribbons? Flowers?" Brenna says, tossing a sock up three times and catching it behind her back as it comes down. Not a miss. Not one. That's coordination.

"Not flowers," says Dini. "They won't last. Ribbons? Don't know. Bells?"

"No," Maddie says. "Can't grab ribbons easily, and

no one will hear them over the music. How about scarves?"

Scarves? "Too traily and wispy," Dini says. "We have to find the right Dolly symbol."

They brood on this awhile, on what would be right for Dolly. Considering how Dolly's characters do the right thing and get their way. That's a hard thing to manage in real life, Dini is coming to see. But it's a goal, she thinks. Something to aim for.

"We need something that means something," says Dini. "An international Dolly symbol." She writes it down quickly: "International Dolly symbol."

But that does not get them any closer to deciding what "it" could be. So they give up and check out the *Filmi Kumpnee* website instead.

From the "News 'n' Views" column of *Filmi Kumpnee: Your Magazine of the Stars* ("Paper? Digital? Our news, you choose."):

> **Dolly fans, we have a word for you, and the word is:**
>
> **Panic.**
>
> ***Filmi Kumpnee's* intrepid reporter has scooped a**

staggering story! Upon arrival in the United States, our own dazzling Dolly narrowly escaped injury in an attack by a wild elephant. Only the swift action of a brave fan saved the day.

Wild elephant, you ask? In America, the land of Hollywood, cowboys, and Citibank? Yes, we asked that too.

But wait! Mr. Soli Dustup himself, manager, owner, and artistic director of Bombay's own Starlite Studios, and patron in chief of the new Bolly-Dazzle Museum, was sighted by a fan at Abu Dhabi Airport catching a connection to Washington, D.C. Our tireless reporter called his mobile number and tried to get a word with him, but "Have to go," that's all he said. So it must be true. Otherwise, why would Mr. Dustup, brave soul, be going in person to America? He knows there is reason to panic.

We are investigating, night and day, across time zones. Stay alert. Thank you to fans worldwide who keep us informed about our starriest star. We

will also be alert, and we'll keep you up-to-date on the latest news—whether breaking or already broken.

No prop help there. "Wild elephant?" says Maddie.

"No way," Dini says. "I saw it. It didn't look even a bit wild to me. Scared, maybe." The *Filmi Kumpnee* people are not as alert as they think they are. In fact, they are out of step. They are not even in the dance.

"Let's go look in my closet," Maddie says.

"For wild elephants?" says Brenna, and they all burst out laughing. Dini tries to stay serious, but she can't.

Chapter Thirty-Five

Brilliant

MADDIE STANDS ON A CHAIR AND HANDS down stuff from the top shelf of her closet, including flags from the collection that she and Dini began together in third grade. "Just put this junk down somewhere so I can see what's up here."

"Does Dolly know the producer guy's coming?" Maddie asks.

"Studio executive," Dini says. "I don't know. I know she was trying to call him."

"Must be really exciting meeting all those movie people," Brenna says, doing a thoughtful handstand.

"It is, sort of," Dini says, trying to twirl the Russian and Sri Lankan flags at once and dropping them both. "Mr. Dustup can be . . . weird sometimes."

"Weird?" Maddie asks, handing down Hawaii and Ukraine. "Like how?"

"It's hard to explain," Dini says. "Just kind of

the way filmi people are, you know? A little . . . clueless." It's not a complaint, just a fact she's never realized before. Grown-ups are supposed to have the answers, but sometimes, she thinks, those filmi grown-ups can be just as clueless as kids.

That includes Dolly. They love her, of course, but let's face it, she's not always what you'd call in touch. It's why she needs loyal fans.

Nepal comes off the shelf, along with Zimbabwe. Brenna says, "Oh, I like that!" The Nepal flag is not rectangular like the others but has unexpected zigzags along one edge. "It matches the steps in the dance."

Dini stares at her.

"What?" says Brenna. "What did I say?"

"Here. Can I show you?" Dini grabs the zigzaggy flag. She does a quick demo, Nepal in one hand and Zimbabwe in the other.

In and out, back and around
and one more loop,
and back and around
and one more loop.

She hands the flags off and shows how the movement begins all over again. "Like that. What do you think?"

"Let me try." Brenna zigzag-loops through the steps at top speed.

She can move fast. She doesn't miss a step! All she has to do is see it once and she's set. Dini can see that Brenna is going to be really, really good at this. Much better than Dini herself, quite honestly.

"Are you all done with your dance?" Maddie's mom demands, emerging from her office room where she fixes clients' accounts.

"Not really," says Maddie, "but we're going out to the front steps."

"Front steps?" says Gretchen.

"Front steps," Maddie says, and hustles them out.

"What's the hurry?" says Dini.

The hurry is about two cans of paint—one green, one silver. "They're left over from the sets we made at school for the end-of-term performance," Maddie explains. "I brought them home for this."

"For what?" says Dini. "I mean, I like the colors. They're—"

"Dolly colors," Brenna says. "Yup. Exactly. See those steps?"

"We're going to . . . ," Dini begins, then stops. "No. Really?"

Maddie nods. Brenna nods. "In case Dolly comes to visit," Brenna says.

"D'you think she *will*?" says Maddie.

Dini is speechless. It's a why-not kind of question, isn't it?

Three steps and some skinny railings may not look like much, but looks can deceive. The painting takes time. Then they have to sit around and watch the paint dry. "Good thing it's not raining," Maddie says.

Dini paints a last stroke. Her hand wavers. The paint pools into a shallow spot where the wood is uneven. "Oops, sorry." She tries to smooth it out but it gets lumpy.

"Here, let me." Brenna takes the brush from her and does some fancy wristwork, and in a quick one-two the lumpy place is fixed.

"How'd you do that?" Dini says. She can hardly see the spot that she'd been on the verge of ruining.

"I have really. Steady. Hands." Brenna puts the brush back in the paint can, then lifts her hand and freezes it in midair. "See? I dare you. Make me move. I can be a statue for*ever*."

"Don't even try," says Maddie. "It's useless, let me tell you. . . ."

Dini looks at Brenna's hand, frozen in front of her face. Brenna is so still Dini can hardly see her breathing. That hand holds completely steady. A statue hand. Brenna shakes loose from the pose. She laughs. "I just can," she says. "Always been that way." She starts on the silver paint now that the green is dry. She paints a zigzaggy silver border on each step. Not a wiggle or a wobble in sight.

Brenna is strange, Dini thinks. But then, sometimes life can use a little stranging up. Look at Dolly. Strange is why she dazzles.

"Hey, girls . . . ?" Maddie's mom, phone in hand, is staring down at their fine handiwork. "What are you doing?!" she demands.

"Surprise!" says Maddie. "Don't you love it?"

Gretchen takes a breath. Then another. "Well, it's . . ." She stops, choosing her words carefully. "Brilliant. That's what it is."

"Do you like it?" says Dini anxiously.

"Let's just say that it might grow on me." Maddie's mom stares at the steps.

"Oh, Mom," says Maddie. "You're not going to make us paint it over, are you?"

Her mother sighs. "No," she says. "But I need

you to promise me, on pain of consequences too terrible to mention, that you're not planning to paint the walls to match."

They promise.

"Your dad called." Gretchen hands the phone to Dini. "He wants you to call him back."

Dini calls Dad. "I'm going out for a while," he says. "Wanted to make sure everything's okay with you."

"Where are you going?" says Dini.

"RadioShack. To buy a coaxial splitter."

Dini has no idea what a coaxial splitter is, although it sounds dangerous. "Don't forget, Saturday is the rehearsal," she says. "And we need to go to Union Station to get some stuff for it in the morning. Flags. Is that okay?"

"Sounds hunky-dory," he says. "See you then, cowhand."

"See you, Dad," Dini says, and hangs up. Her mind is racing faster than she can keep up with it. Maddie and Brenna are laughing together over something. She wonders if they would miss her if she were to sink into those green steps and disappear from sight. She will not, of course. Sinking and disappearing are not normal, everyday actions.

But then she hears what Brenna is saying. "Rehearsal. Grand opening. That's soooo . . ."

"Isn't it just soooo . . . ?" Maddie agrees. "Didn't I tell you Dini was soooo . . . ?"

They stare at her in admiration, which makes Dini feel just a little "soooo . . ." as well, in a funny kind of way. It's nice to be admired, of course, but honestly, it was the last thing she expected. Admiration has just thrown a monkey wrench into her motivation. She didn't exactly plan to be stunned by Brenna. In fact, she came all prepared to dislike her. Not that she wanted to dislike her—or did she? Maybe she did, and that wasn't very nice, was it?

Oh, life is way too confusing, Dini thinks. It is simply impossible to choreograph things like friendship, no matter how hard you try.

Chapter Thirty-Six

The Zoo?

ARRIVING AT THE PROMENADE HOTEL, MR. Soli Dustup tips his helpful cabdriver generously, books himself a room, and falls into the welcome softness of the high-thread-count sheets. Too late to see Dolly now, he tells himself. Tomorrow. Tomorrow.

Mr. Soli Dustup sleeps. And sleeps. He sleeps for several blissful hours. He dreams comforting dreams filled with applause, happy fans, rolling credits, and many, many ticket sales.

But soon the sunlight creeps in through the window and unfurls its warmth across the room, pushing the edge of a shadow right over Mr. Dustup's face. He starts awake, much to his surprise, in the middle of a snore.

Once he realizes where he is, and why, he tries to order breakfast through room service. But it is past noon now and breakfast is no longer being served.

He gets ready in a hurry and hastens to the front desk, where he inquires into Dolly's whereabouts. He offers his business card as proof that he is on the up and up. He can be given this information. He is not some lunatic fan disrupting the star's privacy.

"Mr. Dustup." The hotel manager beams at him. "I know who you are. Mr. Chickoo Dev gave us a list of names so we could screen calls."

Bless that Chickoo. The man is a saint. Dolly is lucky to have found him. "So where's my lovely Dolly, then?" Soli asks, helping himself to a mint from the bowl on the counter. "And my good friend Chickoo? Take me to them." Rested and fortified, he is ready to handle any starry moods in store.

But the manager's reply sends pain knifing up and down Soli's arm. He swallows his mint whole and turns several shades of mauve. "The zoo?" he says. "You took my number one star and you sent her off to the *zoo*?"

"She wanted to go," protests the manager. "On account of the elephant." He launches into a scrambled, tangled story. Dolly is involved, as is an escaped elephant. And Chickoo, who is really okay now, can walk around and everything.

"Why . . . ?" Soli grabs the counter for support. "Could he not walk before?"

The man says something about a dart. No, no, not poison, he hastens to add, but tranquilizer. For the elephant, only it missed the mark.

"Dolly!" exclaims Mr. Dustup, turning fuchsia. "She wasn't hurt, was she?"

"No, no," the manager assures him. "Not Dolly, but Chickoo." He goes into details.

More details than Soli can digest all at once. He waves his arms feebly. He wants to tell this young blabbermouth to hurry up. He wants to know the real scoop, the up-to-the-minute update, the bottom line. Because the thought of Dolly loose in a zoo, with a highly tranquilized Chickoo for company—that thought is turning Mr. Dustup's face from fuchsia to magenta.

Chapter Thirty-Seven

The Zoo!

KRIS HAS TRIED EVERYTHING, BUT MINI won't respond to her favorite toys. She ignores the mobile made out of old pickle barrels. She just sits in the outer room of the Elephant House, ears drooping, emitting the occasional doleful sneeze.

"Peanuts?" Kris offers her a bag of them.

Mini turns away. She gets up and rambles to the door. She bumps it with her head. But the lock has been replaced. That door is no longer an easy exit.

Kris's phone rings. "There's someone here to see your elephant," says the security guard at the main gate.

"No!" Kris snaps. "Tell them we're closed."

"Sorry, she insists. She's come all the way from India and she wants to see Mini again."

"Again?"

"Saw her yesterday."

"On the news," Kris says bitterly, "like half the metro area."

"No, she was there," says the guard. "Listen, give her a minute, will you?"

"Okay, okay," Kris says.

"Name's Dolly. Dolly Singh. She's quite . . . er, unique." He adds something Kris doesn't quite catch, then hangs up.

That can't be right. Did he say she's a famous movie star? Kris shakes her head, braces herself to be polite but firm. No, she will say, you can't come in. The Elephant House is closed for renovation. See that sign?

But when the couple arrives, Kris finds herself rethinking. She's not expecting so much dazzle. Or flying jewelry, or flashing eyes. "What can I do for you?" Kris asks uncertainly. That is not what she meant to say, but the dialogue forms itself.

The man has an amiable smile. His face is, well, dominated by the nose. He introduces himself and the dazzling woman. They're here for a movie opening. "Dolly's latest, greatest hit," he says with pride.

Dolly's latest greatest? So she is. A movie star. She

looks like one. What's more, she knows her own starriness. Kris finds herself wishing she herself were starrier. It would be nice to be starry.

"Is she all right?" Dolly demands. "We saw it all! So much hungaama about a poor little elephant!" She loses a necklace and a ring in her agitation.

Kris has no idea what "hungaama" means, but "poor little elephant" strikes a chord.

"So, what I want to know is," Dolly goes on, "why were those lunatics with dart guns after your precious pachyderm?"

Kris mumbles an explanation about the faulty lock and Mini's escape. She picks pieces of jewelry up and hands them back to Dolly. "You weren't hurt, were you?" she inquires.

"No, but my brave Chickoo was!" Dolly says. "My fiancé, bless him."

"Oh no!" Kris says. This nice guy was the one who got hit?

"Hit by that dart," Dolly says. "Knocked him right out. He crashed like a tree, I tell you."

Kris takes in the meek man with the unruly hair and the nose. He doesn't appear capable of crashing

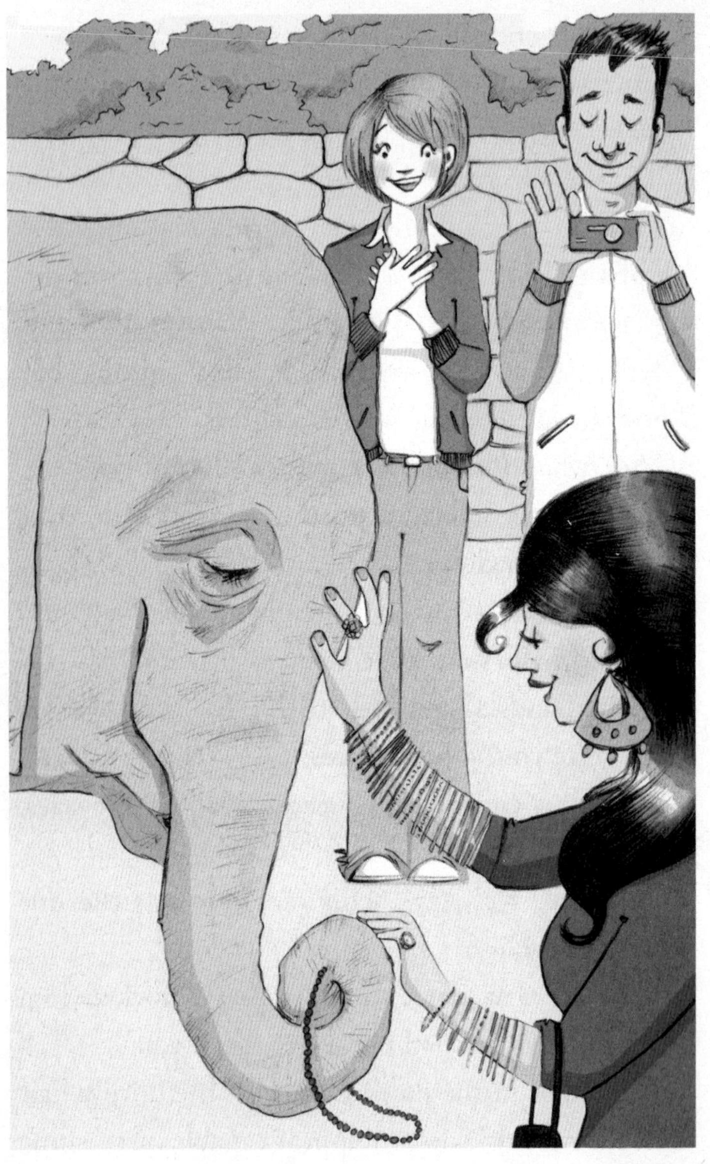

like a tree. "I'm glad you're okay now," she says.

Chickoo scratches his head. "Didn't expect it," he admits. "Took me by surprise."

"So where is your lovely little elephant?" Dolly demands.

"Would you like to see her?" Kris says. These are not the words of a responsible zookeeper. She's not supposed to take them into a closed exhibit. But she is under Dolly's spell. She can't help herself. She thinks, If my boss finds out . . .

Mini's in the outer room. She turns her head when she sees them coming in.

"Oh, pretty princess!" says Dolly.

Mini looks up. She looks up! She hasn't looked at Kris since the business with the dart.

Dolly's necklace flies onto the concrete floor, and Mini gets up. She. Gets. Right up! She ambles gently toward Dolly. She bends and picks the necklace up. Holding it delicately in the end of her trunk, she offers it to Dolly.

"My beauty," Dolly says, and scratches Mini in the wide space between her eyes.

Mini sits. She sits down for Dolly and lets her scratch the top of her head and her flappy ears. She never lets anyone do that but Kris! All of a sudden Kris is filled with hope.

She's glad she didn't turn these nice people away. Look how Mini's relaxing. Look at all the smiles. Listen to the *click-click* of the camera as the man with the nose takes pictures.

But this scene of peace and harmony is about to be rudely interrupted. A red-faced man bursts in, shouting and waving his arms.

Chapter Thirty-Eight

It Takes Three

THE DAY BEFORE THE REHEARSAL COMES upon them like a sneeze—you know when it's about to happen, but it takes you by surprise anyway. It's the beginning of spring break for Maddie and Brenna, so school has let out early on this Friday. Dad is driving the girls to Union Station to buy flags. The front seat is occupied by what looks like the inside of a computer.

"Haan-haan-haan," Dini sings, "nahin-nahin! Kuch to kaho, haan ya nahin."

"What's it mean?" Brenna asks.

Dini knows the answer because she asked Dad and he told her. She noted it down in her green-and-silver stripy notebook and memorized it, because a fan needs to know such things. She says, "Well, it starts out 'Yes-yes-yes, no-no,' right?"

"I got that part," Brenna says, twisting herself into knots. "What comes next?"

It's about halfway through KHSV.

"Dolly's asking him to say something. She's out there in the darkness and it's raining, and she's saying, 'Say yes or no,' you know?" It doesn't come out sounding so great, so Dini tries again. "It's a crisis, see? When she finds her true love, that's when they have the big dance scene in the tea-garden."

"Wow," says Maddie. "True love."

"Can't wait to see the movie," says Brenna. They sigh together in delicious recognition of a great scene. It's a growing-up thing, romance, and in a really good fillum it can get you right where your heart sits.

"So what are these flags for?" Dad wants to know as they turn onto Massachusetts Avenue.

"For the dance," says Dini.

"I see," says Dad with the air of one who does not see at all. He circles back onto a road that looks familiar.

"We just came that way," Dini says.

"I know!" cries Dad, embarking on circle number two.

"So go the other way," Dini says.

"No, no, we have to go this way." Maddie points to a ramp peeling off the main road. "That's the garage entrance."

"Yup," says Dad. "Pretty good, Maddie, for a nondriver."

"Maddie's a human compass," Dini says.

"Oops," says Maddie. "Missed it again."

Dad executes circle number three. "Ha!" He makes it into the parking garage entrance. He grabs a ticket at the automatic gate, which swings up to let them in. "Bull's-eye!" He guns for a space on the second level.

"Well, here we are," he says when they are well parked. "Flag hunting, anyone?"

The shop at Union Station has flags of every country in the world and more. Military flags and sports pennants and historical flags in a vast array of sizes and colors.

The girls buy what they need—Poland, Russia, Bangladesh. Maddie has flags for the other countries Dolly's visited on movie tours. While Dad and the store manager talk excitedly about vexillology (it turns out that is the name for the study of flags), the girls look for a good spot to practice their dance routine.

Behind the fountain will do nicely.

Haan-haan-haan, nahin-nahin, Dini sings, and they try the whole thing again. Yes-yes-yes, no-no! The rhythm of the music pop-snaps into the Union Station shopping complex. Oh, it is just pure Dolly magic. Brenna is good, she picks it up really fast. She even helps Maddie with a couple of the turns.

"Is Dolly really going to rehearse with us?" Brenna says.

"I think so," says Dini. "I hope so." She hums those yeses and noes as she does so, because they help her think. She is thinking at top speed, in fact. The dance is nice, sure. But is it star quality? She can't help remembering that elephant on Connecticut Avenue. She can't help recalling Dolly's cry of happiness when she spotted it.

Wouldn't it be wonderful to get that elephant into the opening? That is a dream, Dini knows. Not very likely. Dad, in his usual punny way, might say it is wildly improbable. But Dini has dreamed of improbable things before.

Sometimes just allowing yourself to dream is half the battle. Not the whole thing, but half. Half is not so bad. It's halfway there. She just has to keep believing it.

Chapter Thirty-Nine

The Cake

CHEF ARMEND IS NERVOUS, A NEW STATE OF being for him. Normally, he is the one who reduces others to a pulp. Now his loyal staff must reassure him that no movie stars are after him.

"She's had lunch, Chef." Alana is doing her best to convince her quaking boss. "She's back in her room, probably getting ready for the rehearsal tomorrow."

"That's right, Chef," says Ollie. He does not mention that he himself sneaked out of the kitchen and got Dolly to sign a menu for him. He does not think the chef would appreciate that.

"Where is this rehearsal?" Chef Armend inquires.

"Must be the Smithsonian," Alana volunteers. "Isn't that where the opening is?"

"Yup," says Ollie. "It's in the paper and everything."

"Heaven help the Smithsonian," mutters the chef.

A knock at the door makes the chef drop a colander.

"I'll get it," says Alana. "Hey there, Miss Curried Soup," she says when she sees who it is.

"I have to talk to the chef," says the girl with the ponytail.

Alana finds herself stepping back. "Come on in." The kid means business.

Dini steps through the august portal of the restaurant kitchen. "Please, Chef," she says, putting on her best manners. "We need your help. Can you make us a really nice chocolate cake? For a couple of hundred people?"

Ollie starts to say something. Alana whispers fiercely and he subsides. Chef Armend gapes at Dini as if he is haunted and she's the ghost responsible.

Dini pushes on. "It's for the movie opening." She has to finish this thought before it frays around the edges, turns to nothing and vanishes with the wisps of steam rising from the cooking pots. She says all in a rush, "And can you add rose petals to the recipe? Please? Dolly's had a really hard time—first she lost her passport—"

Ollie gasps.

"Stop it," says Alana. "What's the matter with you?"

He shakes his head, but he's a quivering custard.

"And the baker who was going to come do the cake for her can't come," Dini carries on, "as if the passport thing wasn't bad enough. So, will you?"

Ollie fidgets. Alana glares at him.

Armend Latifi stares at Dini with quivering eyebrows. He appears to be on the verge of an explosion. Dini practically stops breathing. Oh, this is all going so wrong.

"I, Armend C. Latifi," says the chef, stabbing himself in the forehead with his index finger. Dini winces as if he's stabbed her, which could be next. "I am an artist. Can you comprehend? I make poems of plums. I am a musician of pears, an introspective voyager, heir to shadows and to dreams. Do you understand this?"

"Yes!" Dini cries. "I do! I totally get it!" Does *anyone* get dreams like she does? She doubts it. She's a bit puzzled by the plums and introspective whatnot, but it sounds poetic, which is fine with her.

She feels an odd stirring of sympathy. The chef's a strange person, but Dini gets that, too. His strangeness strikes a chord.

"Ififif I bake this cake . . . ," says Armend, advancing threateningly.

"Yes?" says Dini, backing away.

"Then I will do it my way."

"Of course," Dini says. She's up against the cold steel counter.

The chef stares through Dini at the wall behind her and maybe beyond it to some other place. Seconds tiptoe by. Dini begins to wonder if he's fallen asleep.

"I am of three minds," the chef declares at last.

"Three?" says Dini in alarm.

"Three?" say Ollie and Alana together.

"ThreethreeTHREE," Chef Armend says, banging the counter, so that the ladles skitter madly.

"Okay," says Dini. "Sure. Why not?" She wonders what will happen next. Will Chef Armend sing haan-haan-haan, or nahin-nahin?

He does neither. Instead he utters a single word. "Chocolate."

"Oh yes," says Dini.

"Rose petals."

"Oh yes, yes," she says.

A personal seismic wave overcomes this master of knives, this carver of roasts. Armend Latifi shudders from head to toe and back again. His hat tilts. His shoulders shake.

"Are you all right?" says Dini.

"My grandmother!" the chef says, and dissolves into sobs.

"Where?" says Dini, looking around, half expecting a grandmother to heave into view. But there are still only four people in the sparkly kitchen.

Whisper-whisper, go Alana and Ollie.

"I am heartbroken," says the chef. He collects himself to tell the whole sad story—how his Nona never lived to see his culinary success, how anguish and agony are symbolized by rose petals. "Inscrutable world," he ends, "mythology of myself." He lapses into brooding silence.

But Dini's stuck on a single word. Heartbroken! She never wanted to break anyone's heart. Why, she's all about healing heartbreak, just ask Dolly. "Look, I'm sorry," she says. "I really am." She wants to run out of the kitchen. She thinks, It's all over. What am I going to do about that cake?

And then she thinks one last, frightful thought. I can't do anything right for Dolly's grand opening. "Forget I mentioned it," she says sadly.

"No, wait," Ollie says.

"Chef," says Alana.

"Whatwhatwhat?" says Chef Armend. But he does not shout those words. He does not holler them. Possibly for the first time since he was a young chef, timid and afraid of the experts in the field, Chef Armend lowers his voice. He whispers.

"Why don't you let us help?" Alana says. "Ollie and me, we'll help you make that cake."

"Youyouyou?" muses the chef.

"Yes," say Alana and Ollie.

"Rose petals," the chef says as if he has just discovered that the words have a certain roundness and flavor.

"Yes?" say his three listeners.

"Rose petals," the chef goes on, "have flung themselves into my life too many times. No coincidence. It's a sign." He turns to Ollie. "Youyouyou! Get me a bag of them."

"Rose petals?" says Ollie.

"Nonononono, rabbit ears!" barks the chef, returning to his old self. "Of course rose petals, you butterbrain! NOW!"

"We've got some in the fridge, Chef," Ollie says.

"I need FRESH!" growls the chef, and Ollie hurries out.

Chef Armend's eyebrows dance like animated caterpillars. His chin goes into convulsions. His nostrils flare. His ears twitch. A horrific noise emerges from between his lips. And Dini grins. The cake will be made. All will be fine in this dance that Dini is trying so hard to design and execute. Chef Armend has just chuckled.

"Whenwhenwhen is this . . . this opening?" demands the chef.

Dini gulps. "On the nineteenth," she says. "That's in four days, not counting today."

He purses his lips and glares at the ceiling, then at Dini, and then at that far horizon. "Withwithwith this CAKE," he howls, "I will honor my grandmother!"

Dini and Alana high-five each other in a burst of pure joy.

A great cloud has lifted off Dini's mind. There are still things to be taken care of, but among all the no-noes, here's a ringing yes-yes-yes. It's a turning point, she tells herself, that's what it is.

Chapter Forty

Not Much to Ask For

DINI KNOCKS ON THE DOOR OF ROOM 503, ready to take the grand opening plans to the next step. Ready for Dolly to see their dance and applaud, maybe even help the movements along with a few professional tips. Tomorrow's the dress rehearsal and it's time for action.

Did anyone hear her knock? She can hear voices inside. It's going to be fine, of course it is, especially if everyone pulls together and helps out by watching out. Everyone means everyone, she tells herself firmly. That means they do need the star's help. It's not so unreasonable to ask for it. Is it? She knocks again.

"Come in!" says a chorus of voices, so Dini leans on the door. It opens. She enters.

This is what she hears:

Soli: "But, Dolly darling, I didn't mean—"

Mean what? What is he talking about?

Dolly: "Soli, I was at the zoo, having a wonderful meeting with that precious pachyderm, and you came bursting in and ruined everything! She's a sensitive elephant, you know, and what about *my* nerves?"

At the zoo? Dolly went to the zoo? And Soli? When did all this happen? This dance is getting out of hand.

Chickoo Uncle: "Dolly, maybe we can work something out."

Dini is all for this. Working something out sounds like a very good idea indeed. She takes a quick, sharp look at those assembled.

This is what she sees:

Chickoo Uncle, hovering anxiously.

Maddie and Brenna huddled together on the green velvety sofa.

Soli Dustup, evidently in pain, clutching at his shoulder.

Dolly, waving her hands, so that her bangles go *chan-chan-chan*. Is she dancing? Alas, no.

"Now, you listen to me, Soli my good fellow," Dolly is saying in her silvery voice, which can turn to daggers when weapons are needed. "I don't care how impractical you think I am being. I love that elephant, love her with all my heart and soul! So of course I must have her in my opening. I must. It's not much to ask for, is it? I'm telling you, I can see right away that she's a star."

Soli says something under his breath.

"You should know a star when you see one," Dolly carries on. "Soli, listen to me! If I don't have her at my opening, my heart will break into a thousand pieces. Don't say I didn't warn you."

Chapter Forty-One

Fans

ON THE MORNING OF THE REHEARSAL, WITH a few hours still to go, Dad has errands to run. He gives the grand opening dancers a ride from Maddie's house in Takoma Park to the Metro Center station smack-dab in the middle of D.C., from where they will take the train to the Promenade Hotel. "See you later," Dad says. "Don't go roping any more elephants. Or chefs."

"Very funny," says Dini.

"Dead serious," Dad protests.

They wave good-bye to him and hurry down the steep escalator into the belly of the Metrorail system. The train ride is great fun, especially as there are now Bolly-Dazzle posters in the subway cars and in the station. Dolly's fabulous face floats across those posters, misty hair and sun-sparkly earrings and all. Crowds of Metro riders stop to look at those posters. They linger, point, laugh, talk, and admire. Potential fans, every one of them.

The train is not very full, so they can try their dance steps out in the aisle. "I don't—know," says Maddie, nearly pitching over as they round a bend, "if this is such a wonderful idea. Maybe we should go sit down."

"It's perfect," says Brenna, without missing a step. "Dare you," she says, and dances backward.

They try. Maddie is the first to collapse giggling onto a pale blue vinyl seat. Dini soon follows, flinging herself into a sand-colored one. Brenna could probably do this with her eyes closed.

Not everyone is appreciative of the dancers. "Watch your step," says a woman two rows behind them.

The girls look guiltily at one another, but they can't stop laughing because this has been so much fun.

"Next station stop, Federal Triangle," says the driver's voice.

"Oh, that's us," says Maddie, recovering her breath. "Two blocks to the hotel from here."

With a slowing of wheels and a high-pitched

APRIL
19
Dolly
SINGH

whine, the train stops. "Federal Triangle," the driver's voice proclaims. "Doors open on the right-hand side. Stand clear of the door and watch your step as you exit, please."

"What did I tell you?" demands the cross woman.

The Promenade Hotel has been invaded by reporters, by photographers, and by a gaggle of Dolly fans. They have seen the articles in the *Post.* The special press conference is an added thrill. They have come to see their number one star.

The manager scurries from here to there and back again, doing his best to keep all enthusiastic visitors under control. "Yes, you can take pictures." "Yes, Ms. Singh will be down momentarily." "Just bring your equipment up in the freight elevator." "No! Please don't move the furniture around." "Yes, this is a one-hundred-and-five-year-old building, built by a copper baron in . . ." They follow him in clumps, sticking out their microphones at him, taking pictures with zest and verve.

"Did I tell you about the new museum in Bombay, my dearest friends and Dolly fans?" inquires Mr. Soli Dustup. The fans mill around him like a bunch of sixth graders, talking over one another, laughing at their own jokes, getting Soli's autograph—all this while they wait anxiously for Dolly to make her appearance.

A hotel desk clerk materializes at Soli's elbow and hands him a note. "Message, sir. From the Smithsonian. You may want to check your hotel voice mail. He says he's called a couple of times already."

Soli excuses himself to return that call, leaving Dini, Maddie, and Brenna to the mercy of the fans. A babble of questions breaks out. Yes, Dolly's here, and yes, she'll be down shortly for a brief press conference, and yes, it's true that the events of Dini's life and her meeting with Dolly form a part of the new movie. Yes-yes-yes. With a bunch of make-believe, but haan-haan-haan, there's a little reality in there too.

The questions come full tilt, and the girls learn about the Dolly fans too. Busloads more are on their way from New York, Connecticut, New Jersey, and as far away as North Carolina.

"Is it true you girls are going to do a dance?" someone asks.

"Yes," Dini says. She explains about the opening dance. The grand opening dance. Talking about it to so many admiring fans makes it real somehow. Dini begins to feel faintly starry herself.

But moments like this can be fleeting. This one fades fast into the next dramatic turn, the next quickening of drumbeats.

Only kidding. There should be drumbeats as Mr. Soli Dustup staggers back to the group after his phone call, but life does not always oblige with background music.

Mr. Dustup groans. He manages to pull himself together as Dolly emerges from the elevator and all the fans rush forward. "Array, array, my good people," says Mr. Dustup, elbowing them aside. "Give the star a little breathing room, if you please."

To all appearances, Soli Dustup is once more the competent studio executive dealing with the public who adores his star. But to those who are helping out by watching out, it is clear that something has gone wrong.

"What happened?" asks Maddie.

"It was that phone call," Brenna muses. "He was fine before that."

Dini shakes her head. "Shhh, not now," she says. There are reporters around with cameras, notepads, recorders. She doesn't want their words to show up on tonight's updated *Filmi Kumpnee* website.

One thing is clear. Mr. Dustup has been rattled by that phone call.

Enter Dini's dad, having completed a successful foray into Maryland's suburban shopping jungles for something called a universal adapter. Before Dini can get a word in, Soli corners Dad. They talk in that grown-ups-taking-charge-of-things voice—even though what does Dad know about any of this, and how could he possibly solve whatever new problem has just come up?

"What?" Dini says. "What's going on?"

"Oh, he did?" says Dad to Soli, making warning eyes at Dini. "Who? The caterer? I see. Really? Well, surely there must be—"

Mr. Dustup erupts into an explanation. Words fly through the air. "Messages." "Voice mail." "Smithsonian." "White House." "Canceled."

"Canceled?" Dini can't stand it. Why can't that Soli slow down so she can get what's going on? "White House? What's canceled? Who canceled?"

They stop and look at her.

Dini begs, "Tell us, Dad. Please."

Dad explains that someone from the Smithsonian called Mr. Dustup, that's all.

"Who?" Dini asks. "Why?"

"Really, Dini," Dad says, "it's hard to explain."

"Daddy," Dini reminds him, "you know that when you're fixing a computer and you try to explain it to us and we don't get it, you always say—"

"All right, all right," says Dad. "I know. Patience is the key." And he slows down and lays it out for Dini.

Dolly wanted rose petal milk shakes at the reception. That's all. The museum found a caterer who agreed to supply them, along with other refreshments. Curry puffs. A touch of chocolate in everything. That's all. But now there's a problem, something about a conflict with the Easter Egg Roll at the White House.

So now another caterer must be found. Quickly. A logistical problem, these things happen. And that, says Dad, is absolutely all he knows. He clamps his lips shut to indicate that he is done, done, done.

"What!" Dini and Maddie and Brenna exclaim

in one voice. This is shocking. Hugely horrible. A disaster!

"I'll work on it," says Soli Dustup, heaving an executive-size sigh. "I'll have to break it to Dolly." He and Dad begin to converse again in undertones. Are they talking about the future of rose petals? That is what Dini would like to know, but of course they're not about to tell her. She, after all, is not a grown-up, even though she's been in the double digits for two years now, which should count for something. And didn't she find a baker for that cake when Dolly was in despair, and does anyone even remember that?

Oh, life is very unfair!

Dini says to Maddie and Brenna, "Let's go outside. We have to talk." Talking is good. Talking can solve problems. Only not with a bunch of take-charge grown-ups around.

Chapter Forty-Two

Fan-Sisters

DINI AND MADDIE AND BRENNA ARE DEEP IN conversation as they step along the thyme walkway in the herb garden behind the hotel's Urban Delight Restaurant. A sign invites hotel visitors to step on the thyme walkway. If they do, says the sign, they will release the perfume of the tendrils creeping between the flagstones.

So the girls step and stop. They step and stop and talk at every turn.

"Two problems," says Dini. "We need an elephant. And a caterer."

"That's not all," says Maddie, tripping over a flagstone.

"Steady, Mads," Brenna says.

"Just helping to release the tendrilly perfume," Maddie says, striking a pose. "Listen, fan-sisters—"

"I like that," Dini says.

Maddie grins. "Fan-sisters, we're forgetting a third circle in this dance."

"I know," Dini says. It's been in the back of her mind all the time. "The passport."

A gargling noise to their left makes them wheel around. It is Ollie, in the process of heaving a bag of garbage into the Dumpster that is tastefully hidden behind a hedge. He hurries toward the kitchen, nearly knocking Maddie down. He opens the kitchen door. He vanishes inside.

"What was that all about?" says Brenna, balance-walking along the brick edging of an herb bed.

"I have a funny feeling," says Dini. "Did you see that? I say the word 'passport' and he freaks out."

"You don't think . . . ," says Maddie.

"I don't know," says Dini. "He did that once before. Something's not right with that guy."

"Interesting," says Brenna.

Alana sticks her head out from behind the kitchen door. "What are you guys doing to Ollie?" she demands. "Every time he sees you, he turns into Jell-O. You're not training to be chefs or something, are you?"

"No!" Dini protests. Alana disappears.

"So," says Dini. "We have to think. WWDD?"

"What Would Dolly Do?" Brenna and Maddie intone.

Dolly would keep on going, no question. Dolly wouldn't give up. Dolly would piece the clues together and get the big picture.

"You mean the movie Dolly, right?" says Brenna.

Maddie and Dini trade glances. It's a good question. Which Dolly do they mean? Dini herself has never made that distinction. To her, Dolly has always been Dolly, but she can see Brenna's point.

"The real Dolly's cool too," Brenna says. "Not saying she's not. But you know what I mean?"

"Hmm, yeah, I know," says Dini slowly.

Because while they love the real Dolly, her style and warmth and generosity, it's the movie Dolly who's the heroic one, right? The real Dolly is a person. Well, not a regular person, sure, but still, she's something more than an image floating across a movie screen. And if she's something more, then in a weird and surreal way she's also something less.

The fan-sisters look at one another, trying to connect dots in their minds like tendrils of scented thyme.

Chapter Forty-Three

Rehearsal

ON THE WAY TO THE REHEARSAL DOLLY maintains a somber silence. Chickoo Uncle tries to engage her in conversation, but she will not oblige.

"Not to worry, my darlings," says Mr. Dustup in a fake-hearty voice. "Soli will soon get it all under control."

He has not told Dolly about the caterer catastrophe. Dini thinks they should tell her. She'll find out soon enough. Dini knows from experience that when you try to hide stuff, it all comes out anyway, and then the person you're hiding stuff from gets mad at you. Soli Dustup is a grown-up. Doesn't he know this? And Chickoo Uncle? Why doesn't he tell Soli? What is wrong with all these people? Dad will tell her not to interfere, she knows, but it is hard for a true friend and fan to know what to do. Her instincts tell her it is time to stop being a well-behaved kid. It is time to leap into the fray and become a busybody solving other people's problems.

"It's all going to be fine," says Soli.

Dolly says nothing, just looks out the window as if she is captivated by the streets of D.C. and the Metrobuses with blue and red stripes on their sides and their destinations posted in blinking lights, Pentagon and King Street and Metro Center.

Soli gets quieter. Dad concentrates on driving. In contrast, Dolly perks up when they get to the museum. "Oh, look at those gates!" She clasps her hands in admiration at the stonework in the garden outside the Smithsonian's Sackler Gallery.

"They're moongates," Brenna tells her. "Look, you can follow the trail between them, that way, and then back again to the street exit."

"I adore these moongates," Dolly declares. "Chickoo, we must get a pair for the garden at Sunny Villa."

"Yes, Dolly," says Chickoo Uncle meekly.

"We'll get a pair for the Bolly-Dazzle Museum as well," Mr. Dustup declares. "You want moongates, Dolly darling? You shall have them."

Dolly picks up the hem of her leaf-green skirt with the silver edging and dances up to one of those gates along the garden path. She stops and turns in the middle of the rounded cutout space between its two halves.

"Haan-haan-haan," Dolly sings in a thoughtful kind of way. "Nahin-nahin. Does anyone have a map of the area?"

"I do," says Maddie. "I always carry it with me."

"Excellent," says Dolly briskly. "You never know when you'll need a map. May I?"

"Sure," says Maddie. She pulls the map from her backpack and gives it to Dolly.

Then Dolly and her dance troupe of three, along with tech support (Dad, Soli, and Chickoo Uncle), enter the domed lobby of the Sackler Gallery to rehearse the opening dance.

Mr. Dustup offers Dini a small package. "For you," he says. "Trailer and rough cuts of the opening song sequence."

"From KHSV?" says Brenna in awe.

"Stunning," says Maddie.

"Yes, yes, the very same, my darlings," says Mr. Dustup. "Just for you devoted fans."

Dini puts the DVD away carefully in her backpack so it doesn't get lost in the confusion. All around them the gallery, that treasure trove of Asian art, is being turned upside down. Not physically, no, no. The taxpayers of America would not stand for that. But on this breezy spring evening it is humming and thrumming in anticipation of the grand event to come.

Chairs are being arranged in concentric circles in the lobby. Sound equipment is being tested. Signs are being placed strategically in alcoves, showing the way:

BOLLY-DAZZLE!

An extravaganza of films from India

Grand Opening: *Kahan Hai Sunny Villa?*

(Where Is Sunny Villa?)

Opening dance by young performers.

Music. Refreshments. Fun.

Special Guest: Dolly Singh

The young performers practice their twirls and swirls under the ornate domed ceiling of the Sackler's lobby. Their green and silver skirts swish.

The flags in their hands sweep in and out, in and out, forming repeating arcs of a circle. Their ankle bells jingle and jangle. Dolly gives them pointers.

"Like this, my sweet girls," she says, showing them how to make flowers, arrows, whirling weapons just by using their hands. How to stamp-stamp-stamp their feet to create rhythms within the larger pattern of the dance-two-three,

and one-two-three,

and repeat-two-three,

and back-two-three.

"Very pleasing and poetic," Dolly says. "A marvel of magical movement." She claps her hands in delight. She is so much more dazzling when she's delighted.

Off they go, again and again and back again and yet again. It's good. It is. It works. All the planning.

Mr. Dustup offers a few technical bits of advice. "Enter from left stage," he suggests, "and then circle back so that you can exit in the opposite direction." He draws sweeping lines in the air to show what he means. "A little visual variety works wonders. It will keep you on your toes, and the audience also. Trust me, audiences like to be given patterns to work with in their subconscious minds."

All the practice. All the worry. It finally works.

Dad and Soli Dustup applaud. "Encore!" says Dad, and of course they oblige.

"Array vah, my darlings," says Soli when at last the dancers are breathing heavily and taking endless turns rehydrating themselves at the water fountain. "You are stars. You should be in the fillums."

"Really?" says Maddie, mopping her face with her T-shirt sleeve.

"Anytime you want to be in a dance scene, you just get in touch with Soli Uncle."

Dad coughs and murmurs something about school and getting an education first.

"Of course, of course, there is no conflict there," agrees Mr. Dustup. "Just remember, if we ever do a shoot on summer break, you're in. Shame to waste such talent. Our Dolly herself, you know, made her first movie when she was only—what? Eleven? Twelve? Something like that. Just a blinking child, she was."

Which is when Dini realizes something. She hasn't seen Dolly in a while. Not since she showed them all that hand movement stuff and they went stamp-two-three and one-two-three together, which was way glorious, but where'd she go after that?

Where is Dolly now? Has anyone seen the star?

April 16, 2011

Darling Chickoo,

Writing this in a hurry because there's no time. Soli's being stubborn. He won't listen to me. If he won't trust me, his number one star, who can he trust, I ask you? "Dolly," he keeps saying, "this is America, you can't just get elephants whenever you feel like it." So little faith, I tell you.

So I am going off on a small errand by myself. Where there's a will, Chickoo . . . We know that, don't we? You're always saying if you really want something done, you have to do it yourself. So I'm dashing off to do this thing myself. I have high hopes, my dearest. The grand opening of KHSV must be as terrific and tremendous as possible. It must be magical and magnificent.

Don't worry about me. I have a map.

Love,
Dolly

Chapter Forty-Four

Rattled

"WHAT WAS I THINKING?" SAYS CHICKOO Dev. He is holding a note in his hand and looking decidedly rattled. "I should have known something was up when she said she wanted to go out in the garden."

"It's not your fault," Dini says.

"Why would she want to be out in the garden instead of inside supervising the arrangements?" Chickoo asks. "I should have guessed she had something in mind. Oh, Dolly, Dolly."

"I saw her going out," says Brenna, twisting her arms around each other and clasping her hands together. "I thought she was just going to dance through the moongates."

"She doesn't know anything about gardens," says Chickoo, sinking further into despair.

A couple of people from the administrative office

of the Smithsonian have entered the scene. They are talking animatedly about a server problem and e-mails, as if that has anything to do with Dolly's disappearance.

Dini wishes they would take their servers and e-mails somewhere else. She is hot on the heels of a solution to this latest problem, and an idea has just clicked open in her mind. "Dad," she asks, "can you take us to the zoo?"

"The zoo?" says Dad.

"Girlie," says Mr. Dustup in admiration. "You took the words out of my mouth. That was my thought precisely."

"Ah, I see," says Dad. "The zoo it is, then."

Soli slaps Chickoo Uncle on the back, sending him reeling. "Fear not, Chickoo my friend," he says, "you're in good hands. Would I let anything happen to our sweet Dolly?"

Chickoo Uncle looks as if he does not know how to answer that question.

"What?" says Mr. Bayan, that beleaguered and high-ranking official at the Smithsonian Institution. "What do you mean the server is down?"

"That's what they told me," his secretary says. "They got flooded with e-mails from California and New York and Texas. The system crashed."

"California? New York?"

"Yes, Mr. B. Turns out this movie star—Dolly Singh—has a big fan base in the Bay Area and Queens. And Houston. It was the Texas batch that finally crashed the server." She frowns. She has never liked Texans, and these crashing e-mails just confirm her feelings about them.

She tries to be diplomatic. "They're quite upset." She swallows her true sentiments. In her opinion, the fans are not "quite upset." They are raving mad. They are lunatics. According to the morning paper, they're demanding that the US government release Dolly. They think she's being held hostage. They're ranting about stolen passports.

But she does not say all that. It's too hard to explain such complicated happenings.

Mr. Bayan emits an exasperated snort. He is starting to wonder if this whole film festival was a bad idea from the start. He thought he'd gotten Dolly sorted out. Now some news item about her passport has ruined everything.

The State Department has been calling. The Indian ambassador has sent her assistant over a couple of times. They are all offering advice, suggestions, help. But he—Rolando Bayan, of the United States Marines (retired), program director of educational and cultural events at the Smithsonian—is in charge, and frankly, he is annoyed. He does not need help. He needs order!

And now these freaky fans. Military combat, he thinks irritatedly, was more organized than this . . . this opening!

To make it even worse, this Dolly person has disappeared. If he finds her, he's going to give her a reprimand. He's going to make her understand that she has wrecked his day.

And yet, and yet. When he heard the music playing in the lobby of the museum today, when he saw those kids practicing their dance, it did something to him. It made him want to clap his hands and stomp his feet. The grand opening is threatening to fall about his ears, yet Mr. B. gets a warm and dancy feeling when he hears those Dolly tunes.

Chapter Forty-Five

Falling Star

TARIQ HASAN, PROUD BANGLADESHI AMERICAN, father of twins, and taxi driver with the National Limo & Cab Company, can hardly believe his luck.

"Hey, Tariq, buddy," his friend Dave had said through the crackle of the dashboard speaker, "guess who your next fare is? Remember I told you about that movie star, Dolly? . . . Yeah, herself. She needs a ride. . . . Yup, right now. Can you take her to the zoo?"

Dolly Singh? Herself? Is such coincidence possible? Call it kismet. Call it fate. Call it the improbable becoming gloriously possible, as it does in the finest fillums. So Tariq wends his way through Arlington, Virginia, and hops on 395 into the District. Following the signs to the National Mall, he arrives shortly at the back entrance of the Sackler Gallery to pick up this very important passenger.

"Dolly-di," he says now, using the form of address his language employs for a respected sister. "Is it really you? I heard you sing in Dhaka when you did your South Asian tour."

Dolly assures him that she is indeed herself. Who else could she be? "Take me to the zoo, my friend," she says. "I'm looking for an elephant."

Dini's father dodges the cars and trucks and vans on the roads of Washington. He navigates an endless series of traffic lights, all bent on turning red just as he pulls up. But he sticks with it, and soon they are turning into the parking lot at the National Zoo. That is not soon enough for some of his passengers, but that's how life is, full of missed beats.

Now they emerge to race to the Elephant House, arriving collectively out of breath. A small group of fans is already keeping Dolly on her toes.

Mini is there, along with the other elephants, in an enclosure with a high Plexiglas wall separating them from the humans. Her cold now cured, she no longer needs to be alone. She's up against the Plexiglas, waving her trunk and waffling for attention. People! Mimi likes people.

Kris is there, looking confused.

"Chickoo darling," says Dolly. "Are you okay? Didn't you get my note?"

"Oh, Dolly," says Chickoo weakly, "I was so worried."

"Oh, Chickoo," says Dolly.

"Oh, Dolly," says Chickoo.

Dini knows they can go on this way for quite a while, so she coughs politely to remind them there are steps to be danced.

Also present is a cabdriver named Tariq Hasan. He, too, is a fan. "I'm so grateful to my friend Dave," he says to Dolly, "for putting me in touch with you. Such a gift. Truly, meeting you is the aloo in my singara, the macch in my jhol."

Dolly, unfazed at being compared to the potato in a pastry or the fish in a curry, declares, "Friendship is an emerald in the necklace of life." She explains to everyone how she came to have Tariq as her driver—a fan, of all things, in this country so far from India-where-the-fans-all-live. It's a complicated plotline, full of twists and turns, like one of Dolly's movies. Tariq's friend is that same driver in whose taxi Maddie was squished and Dini was knocked breathless by a suitcase. The best dances come from such intersecting movements.

"And fans are the jewels in a star's night sky," concludes Dolly in a poetic burst.

Maddie gets the connections too, Dini can see. A memory surfaces instantly between them, of flying bags in a crammed taxi. "This whole elephant thing started in Dave's cab," Maddie says.

"I guess so," says Dini.

"Great minds follow the same trails through life's forest," Dolly says vaguely.

"Who's Dave?" says Brenna, confused, so they have to explain the story line to her all over again. She's not yet used to the twisty story lines of Dolly's life.

At the time, Dini wished that she hadn't put ideas of parades and elephants into Dolly's head. But now here is an elephant and there is the opening, coming up so very soon. It makes perfect sense to synchronize the two. Why not?

But in every dance routine there are false steps to correct. Kris's boss is stepping out of tune. "No elephant of ours is going to be in a parade," he says. "It's out of the question. We are a zoo, not a circus."

"Elephant rodeo?" Dad mutters.

"Daddy," says Dini.

"Sorry, couldn't help it," says Dad.

"I remember going to the circus as a slip of a boy . . . ," Mr. Dustup begins, rising partially from the bench over which he has draped himself.

"Not now, Soli," Dolly hisses. He subsides.

"It might be fun," Kris says. "It would cheer Mini up for sure."

"She'll be fine when all this is over," says her boss, waving his hands at the remains of the construction—unfinished ceilings and piles of boxes and debris outside the building.

"Oh, must you be so cruel?" Dolly demands, flinging a bangle up in the air.

The bangle flies over the Plexiglas partition. Mini catches it tidily. She juggles it with glee. She tosses it up, catches it as it comes back down, and ends the routine with a pleased snuffle.

"Stunning!" the girls chorus. The zoo director, Kris's boss, glares at them.

Mr. Dustup awakens suddenly. He stands up from his bench. He stretches. He wiggles his ears. He practically glows around the edges, as if a sudden fire has ignited in his studio executive mind. "What

PR," he murmurs. "Think of it. Everyone will know that your elephant was at a Dolly opening."

He says it softly, but the words leave traces of themselves in the high-ceilinged interior of the Elephant House. Dolly-Dolly-Dolly, go the echoes. Opening-ning-ning.

"You think so?" says the zoo director, snapping to alertness himself.

"Yes-yes-yes-yes-yes-yes!" choruses his audience, Dini and Maddie and Brenna and Chickoo Uncle and Mr. Soli Dustup and Tariq the cabdriver. Mini wiggles her ears.

"People will flock to your zoo," says Mr. Dustup, hitting his stride. "You will have donations. Your memberships will rise. Fame." He throws his arms wide open. Dini throws her arms wide too in that Dolly gesture.

So do Brenna and Maddie. Three pairs of arms fly up in synchrony. Perfect.

"Maybe," says Chickoo Uncle, piping up, "someone will want to make a movie here."

The zoo director whips his head around, listening to these suggestions with light dawning all over his face.

"Why not?" It's Soli's turn. "Anything's possible."

"We can tell *Filmi Kumpnee,*" Dini says. "They'll be happy."

"Who's that?" says Kris, puzzled.

Dini explains about the fan magazine and website, whose reporters and editors have been worried about Dolly and have been communicating that worry to fans worldwide.

"Worldwide?" says the zoo director.

"Worldwide," says Mr. Soli Dustup. "Let me tell you, my good man, all about the Bombay fillum business. But first you must understand that the matter of the elephant is really very easily accomplished. Look here, they don't call me the Visualizer for nothing. . . ."

The entire troupe then exits to the elephant yard, where Kris lets Mini and the other elephants out into the newly constructed run (now well secured at all exits) for their evening exercise. Meanwhile, Mr. Dustup has the zoo director firmly by the arm. He is walking him through his visualization of Dolly's grand opening, and Kris's boss is nodding, nodding. He is mesmerized by Mr. Dustup.

Is it a filmi thing? Will Dini be able to hold an

audience that way someday? What a thrilling thought. It makes her feel slightly heroic.

Dusk falls. The pleasant landscape blurs gently into darkness. "Oh, look at that!" Dolly points to the sky. "A falling star!"

"To be precise, a shooting star," Dad says. "A meteorite."

"Mostly I prefer my stars to rise," says Mr. Soli Dustup, blowing an affectionate kiss at Dolly.

Chapter Forty-Six

Alert!

AND SO THIS LONG DAY COMES TO AN END, this day that is three days short of the grand opening, this day filled with flags, cakes, rehearsals, elephants, arguments, and missing and shooting stars. Its beat is well timed, its rhythm has slowed and gentled, and all our heroic participants are ready now for a well-earned rest.

Alas, that is not to be. Even the best-rehearsed dance routine may be brought to disaster by an object left carelessly onstage. In this case, by an object left at the top of the stairs, where a person could easily trip over it and come crashing down.

The object is a backpack.

The person is Maddie.

Having gone to check the *Filmi Kumpnee* website for updates, and having found a most alarming one, she prints it out and rushes for the stairs, to join her mother and Dini and share this new development with them. But she forgets one thing that the *Filmi Kumpnee* people keep stressing in all their columns. She forgets to be alert.

Maddie was not supposed to trip and fall. Tripping and falling was not a part of the choreography for the grand opening dance. But trip Maddie does. She falls. She yowls in agony.

A couple of hours later in the nearest urgent-care facility, it is established that she has broken a toe. The pinkie toe on her right foot. She is sent home with her toes taped together and her foot encased in an ugly, square orthopedic shoe. No dancing, she has been told. Dancing is not in her immediate future.

Here is the cause of this tragic event—from the "News 'n' Views" column of *Filmi Kumpnee: Your Magazine of the Stars*:

> **Faithful fans of our own oh-so-fabulous Dolly Singh, take note. An inside source sends us word from America, where our Dolly is visiting. The word is . . .**
>
> **False accusation!**

Yes, we know that is two words, but wait. Unnamed people are accusing us of stealing Dolly's things to sell on the Internet. Our reputation is at stake, just when we have big plans. Big plans to enhance and enrich a major artistic collection.

"What?" you cry. We cry too. Our tears are flowing, we can assure you. Copiously.

But what is the use of crying? We must do something. And we will. We will confront our accuser and clear our good name.

Meanwhile, Dolly fans, unite to help us gather round our star. Go to Washington, D.C., to support her at the grand opening of KHSV. We, too, will do our best to send our fearless reporter.

We are ever alert, so you be alert too. Watch this spot for the latest in this thrilling saga of world travel and conquest.

Dini reads the printout sadly. She wonders, What plans? What collection? Those questions fade because there are so many others that need Dini's attention. Too many, all at once. To think she imagined herself to be even slightly heroic. The problem with that, she can see, is that heroes get stuck with having to find answers to the tough questions when no one else can. That thought settles inside her like a particularly heavy and uncomfortable rock.

Chapter Forty-Seven

Sleuths

MADDIE'S MOM UNFOLDS THE FUTON IN THE family room and makes a bed there so Maddie doesn't have to walk upstairs.

"I'll bring the sleeping bag for me," Dini says.

"Maybe I should sleep down here, Dini," Gretchen says, "in case she needs anything at night."

"Mom, no!" Maddie says. "I'll be okay."

"I'll come get you if she needs anything," Dini promises.

Gretchen hovers and hovers for ages before she finally turns the light off and leaves them alone. It is now past midnight, a whole new day, but the awful thing that has just happened is only now beginning to sink in.

"Does it hurt?" Dini asks as Maddie fixes the pillow under her foot.

Maddie wrinkles her nose and purses her lips and

says, “Nah, not really,” which doesn’t sound very convincing.

Then she says, “We need to talk to him. That Ollie guy. He knows something. Maybe it’s him. Maybe he’s got her passport.”

“I’ll call the restaurant,” says Dini. “Tomorrow morning, first thing.”

“Sleuths,” Maddie says, stretching her arms above her head and watching the shadows on the wall. “We need to be sleuths.”

“We do,” says Dini. “Look, I’ll call him and talk to him or to that woman—Alana. I bet she knows. Maybe she can get him to return the passport to Dolly. *If* he’s the thief.”

“I think he is,” Maddie says. “Who else could it be?”

“I don’t know. I think we should do this right. Check all the options. Sort of like Dolly does in KHSV, you know what I mean?”

Maddie gets very quiet.

“What do you think?” says Dini.

But Maddie is not listening. The painkillers have done their job and knocked her out. Maddie has fallen asleep.

Chapter Forty-Eight

Breaking News

NO-NO-NO!

This is terrible. It is worse than elephants on the loose. Much worse than the little matter of finding a person to bake a cake. Maddie's falling down the stairs gives new meaning to the phrase "breaking news." Sleuthing is a whole lot tougher when one of the sleuths is blurry eyed from painkillers.

The breaking news has kept Dini awake. She couldn't sleep all night, and now it is early morning. She tries closing her eyes, but patterns circle in her mind like dance steps, looping back on themselves over and over until Dini's dizzy. She turns over and back and over again. It's no use. She bunches the sleeping bag around her because she's cold, then flings it off again because she's hot.

She remembers something that she can and should do. Right now. She can't sleep anyway, so why not?

She tiptoes to the computer room, expecting to find it empty, but Gretchen is there already, tidying up.

"Can I just do one quick thing?" Dini asks. "It's really important."

"Now? It's not even six a.m.," says Gretchen, but she turns the computer on before heading to the kitchen in pursuit of her morning coffee.

Dini pulls up the White House website and clicks her way to the "Contact Us" page.

She fills in all the required fields, using Maddie's address and contact information so that the president knows she's close by and not writing all the way from India. Then she types her message into the box with its warning: "Please limit your message to 2,500 characters."

Dear Mr. President,

My name is Nandini Kumaran, but my friends call me Dini. I am a big fan of the Indian movie star Dolly Singh, and my friends Maddie and Brenna are too. We are having a grand opening of Dolly's movie at the Smithsonian. Now the caterer has dumped us because they're going to be doing the White House Easter Egg Roll instead and have to be at a meeting the same time as our grand opening. That is a little unfair. I don't know what you can do, but I wanted to let you know.

Sincerely,

Dini Kumaran

She pauses to consider how to count the characters in that message. Does 2,500 mean with spaces or without? She counts both ways and breathes easy. That is 407 characters without spaces and 504 with. "Piece of cake," she whispers, channeling Dad.

She clicks "Contact me" and types the phrase in the prompt box. It says "from. msSteps," whatever that means. She checks to make sure her case and punctuation match the prompt. This will prove to the president that she is a human being and not a spambot. Then she hits "Submit" and relaxes as the confirmation page pops up. "Thank you!" it says.

It goes on to assure Dini that she can indeed help the president to secure the future of America. She is not sure she's doing that exactly, but the bold letters and the friendly exclamation point are a comfort.

"Are you done?" Gretchen says, returning with a bitterly fragrant cup of coffee. "Go back to sleep, you. You don't need to be up for a while yet."

Dini leaps up from the chair and throws her arms around Gretchen's neck. "Oh, thank you, thank you!" she cries.

"You're welcome," says Maddie's mom, surprised.

When Dini gets back to her sleeping bag on the floor of the family room, she finds Maddie murmuring, "One, two, three. One-two-three, one-two-three, one-two."

Oh no! In her sleep Maddie's thinking of the one thing that she can't do—dance. It's so unfair. Can't toes be designed better so they don't just snap when a person loses her balance and falls down a few stairs? Way too many things still need Dini's attention—cakes and catering and passports. She does not need toes on that list.

What's more, Maddie's trying so hard to be brave.

"Does it hurt?" Dini kept asking the night before. To which Maddie scrunched up her face, chewed her lip, and said, "No, not really. Not so badly." That was clearly not true at all.

Now, in her sleep, Maddie's still trying. Dini's heart feels slightly fractured out of sympathy.

Another thought tugs at her. Will the dance even work with only two people in it? Brenna's very good, but still, how do you trace a pattern that's supposed to go in circles when you have only two dancers onstage? There's no time now to change the whole thing.

Maybe it doesn't matter, she tells herself. Mini and Dolly will steal the show, so maybe no one will pay attention to that opening dance. Fans will come to see Dolly, to hear her sing, to attend the premiere of her latest, greatest movie. They will not come to see two kids putting on an opening dance.

Which is fine. Isn't it? Of course it is. Dolly's the star. That's the way it's supposed to be.

And yet, and yet . . . why does that thought jab Dini with its sharp little needles? Why does it deflate her, make her spirits sink and sink some more, until she feels as if she's falling away from her hopes and dreams and plans, yes, plans? This trip was going to be so much fun, and now it's become a disaster with broken bones and stolen passports dancing everywhere.

Chapter Forty-Nine

Grimaces

SUNDAY DAWNS FINE AND MILD, WITH FLUFFY clouds drifting happily through a clear blue postcard of a sky. Birds are chirping. Squirrels are scurrying. Azalea bushes have burst forth in scarlet and pink and purple bloom. Nature seems to be busy scattering promises of happiness everywhere.

Dad calls to see how Dini is doing. She tells him the dreadful news about Maddie's foot. He is sorry, he says, and do they need any help?

Well, they need Maddie's toe to be fixed, but there is nothing Dad can do about that, so Dini says, "No, I don't think so."

"Too bad about Maddie's accident," Dad says. "Just have to tape it up and let it heal." Then he tells her that the people at the B&B could use some help with their satellite connection, so he may be spending the morning on their roof. Fixing wires is

Dad's idea of fun, and the fineness of the day has inspired him. If Maddie's foot had wires in it, Dad would probably leap to the task.

Maddie's mom gets on the phone and tells Dad that everything is under control and he should go ahead and make his plans. What on earth can she mean? Nothing is under control. Nothing!

In Dini's opinion, it should be cloudy and rainy. Cloudy and rainy would fit the mood better. All that happy-chirpy blue sky, it's a big fraud.

Back in the family room that also doubles as random storage space, Maddie's mom fusses over Maddie.

"Mom," Maddie says, "you checked that tape already."

"Does it hurt?" Gretchen asks.

"No," says Maddie, clenching her teeth as she puts on the ugly, square black orthopedic shoe with the hard sole and Velcros it in place. Dini finds her own teeth gritting in sympathy.

Maddie's mom leaves with a last rush of concern.

Dini picks up the X rays from the end table and holds them up to the light. Maddie looks away.

X rays are so weirdly spooky. Dini shivers at

the thought of pictures that cut right through the outside and go all the way to the bone. This one shows the bones of Maddie's right foot. The smallest one on the very end has a fine thread of a crack zigzagging across it. The toe is sticking out a bit, which is why it has to be taped up to the rest of Maddie's foot.

Dini considers the informational sheet that accompanies the X ray. It labels the bones of the foot. They look all Halloweeny and skeletal, which of course they are. "It's called a distal phalanx," she says. "That bone in your little toe."

Maddie groans, as if the technical name of her bone is a source of distress. "I feel so dumb," she says. "If you're going to break something—a toe? I mean, really."

"Want to watch the KHSV video?" Dini says, trying to cheer her up.

"It's humiliating," says Maddie.

Dini puts the DVD in and clicks to the right place. She is glad to see Maddie brighten up just a little as the trailer comes on.

Look at those tea-gardens! Hear the silvery *chan-chan-chan* of jewelry falling to the ground. And the music, fading away: "Haan-haan-haan, nahin-nahin!" Dini hums along and Maddie manages to join in. A zigzag crack in the distal phalanx of the little toe can't stop you from humming.

Maddie clicks forward to the rough cuts of the title song. There are three versions: one with a couple of stanzas missing, one with some extra musical to-ing and fro-ing, and one that is close to the final scene. Here Dolly drops her cell phone while she's getting out of a little yellow electric car.

"Look," says Maddie. "What's she doing?" They rewind Dolly and there goes that phone again.

"That's pretty much what happened in real life, too," Dini says. So much of this movie is based on things that happened to Dolly in real life. Dolly's life. But also Dini's life, when they met in faraway Swapnagiri.

In that song sequence Dolly's phone falls right out of her generously sized purse. It falls into the car. It slides under the seat and out of sight. Dolly proceeds to sing her song.

Dini and Maddie look at each other. A real-life scene zips into focus in Dini's mind, a scene with a different setting, another car. A taxi, right here in Washington, D.C. Outside the Promenade Hotel in this quick flashback, the cab stops. The luggage quits slamming into Dini. Everyone gets out. Dolly. Dini. Maddie. The cabdriver.

"Did it fall out of the taxi?" Dini says.

"Could be," says Maddie.

They play the movie scene again. The image of the filmi car, with something falling out of the purse, slip-slides over the memory, so that real real and movie real—call it surreal—are all mixed up. Two minds trying to focus on the same shared memory. Isn't that what friendship is about?

"So maybe that Ollie guy picked it up," Maddie says. "And is trying to sell it?"

"Maybe," says Dini. But that doesn't sit right somehow. That Ollie guy, tripping over his feet and gargling, couldn't audition for a villain role to save his life. "I'll go call him," Dini says.

"Taste," says Chef Armend. "Tastetastetaste." An array of miniature cake samples are laid out on elegant platters upon the kitchen counter. "Come on, come on. Tell me what you taste."

He has worked on these samples for hours.

He has tried many different recipes. Now he is practically prancing around the kitchen of the Urban Delight.

Ollie is staring at the cakes as if he expects them to get up and start walking around. "Come on, Ollie," Alana prompts him. "Dig in!"

He does, but he seems preoccupied.

Those samples look delectable. They taste every bit as fine. The cake is moist. The chocolate flavor is rich and smooth. And what is that undertone? "Lavender?" says Alana cautiously.

The chef nods. An unaccustomed grimace spreads over his face. Chef Armend is smiling a lot today.

"Rinse. Spit," he orders, pushing a bucket toward them. "You want to cultivate your palate, my young barbarians!" Alana obeys, getting one flavor out of her mouth before sampling another.

Ollie's still staring off into space. She nudges him and he snaps to the task.

"Pineapple?" Ollie ventures.

Alana tries some. "Yes, and a touch of vanilla. Wonderful, Chef. I never would have thought of combining those with chocolate."

Chef Armend rubs his hands.

"Jasmine," says Alana, trying the next one. "And green tea? It's divine."

"Very good, my fine people," proclaims the chef. Who knew they were ever his fine people? He draws a final platter out from the array behind him. "Now this one."

Forks clink. Eyes widen. Taste buds dance in delight. "Mmm," Ollie and Alana say together.

"Rose petals," says Alana. "With something else—lemon verbena, I think. Brilliant!"

The chef clears his throat. "Whywhywhy not?" he says. "Have to move with the times. No harm being a bit . . . experimental." He picks up a sample and pops it into his own mouth, chews, swallows, and there is that grimace of happiness again. "I," he says, "will bake this cake for that movie star's grand opening. You can tell her that." He kisses his fingertips. "And for my Nona," he adds.

The phone rings, making Ollie jump.

Chef Armend answers it himself. Remarkably, he says "yes" many more times than "no." The only time he says "no," in fact, he follows it up with, "I don't mind. Why would I mind? Goodgoodgood."

Something is happening to our tyrannical chef.

Chapter Fifty

Tell Her!

"OLLIE," SAYS ALANA AS THEY'RE MEASURING and mixing. "I need to talk to you."

Ollie drops his spatula. "What? About what?"

"About you," says Alana. "Why are you acting like a quivering soufflé?"

"Who, me?" says Ollie, looking around nervously.

"Yes, you. Fess up. What's on your mind? You've been acting so guilty, anyone would think you've stolen the Washington Monument. Oh, stop wringing your hands like that, you're making me dizzy."

Ollie stops, mesmerized. Alana's so efficient. She's as sharp as a set of good knives. But she's kind. He's never noticed that before. That, right there, is a kind look.

Kind looks have a way of making the truth come bubbling up. It does so now. Ollie tells her all. His Internet search, his discovery of the website selling the passport, and the nasty people whose Tweets gave him the screaming heebie-jeebies.

"And the worst thing is," he concludes, "that I looked up that website on my cell phone. On my break just now."

"Yes? And what did you find?" She taps her foot impatiently.

"It's sold, Alana!" he wails. "They sold it in an auction on that movie website. Someone's bought Dolly's passport! And I sent the website an e-mail protesting, you know, because I couldn't stand that they'd sold it—and oh, Alana! They yelled at me."

"In an e-mail?" she says, puzzled.

He nods miserably. "All caps," he whispers.

Alana looks as if she wants to say something more, but the phone rings, so instead she answers it. "Yes," she says. "Well, okay, but you'll have to make it quick. We're very busy right now." To Ollie she mouths, "Two minutes."

He nods humbly. Two minutes? He could wait for her for hours. If she told him to leap off a cliff, he'd gladly leap.

Thankfully, no leaping is required. She's off the phone faster than Ollie can say "panini press." What is she going to say? Will she think he was snooping? That it's none of his business what happens to Dolly's passport? That he should quit wasting his time?

But Alana doesn't say any of those things. Instead she bursts out laughing! She doubles up from laughing. She has to clutch at her side.

"What's so funny?" says Ollie, affronted.

"You!" Alana gasps. "The kids thought it was you who stole the passport!"

"Me!" says Ollie. "I would never . . ." He stops, because who knows, really? If he'd found it, what would he have done? Who knows?

She calms herself. "I wouldn't have picked you to play virtual gumshoe. Ollie, I swear, you surprise me."

"I do?" says Ollie, shocked.

She wipes her eyes. "Of course, you'll have to tell her what you've found out," she says. "I don't know why you didn't say anything. To me? To her? To anyone."

As if it were so easy. What will Dolly say to him? How long have you known about this? And you're coming to me now? Are you sure it wasn't *you*? Did you steal it? Or did you buy it?

He laughs what he thinks is a bitter laugh, but it comes out in an anguished gurgle. It is one thing to be yelled at by your boss, quite another to be the target of a famous movie star's wrath.

"You didn't do anything wrong," Alana says.

He stares at her. She repeats, "You didn't. Do anything wrong. Just remember that."

That is true. He didn't, did he? So why is he acting guilty? Get a grip, Ollie, he tells himself. Alana's right! Her words sink in. He didn't do anything wrong. He wants to shout for joy.

"Thank you, Alana, oh thank you," he says in a rush of gratitude. "You're so clever."

"Oh no," says Alana modestly.

"And so good . . ."

"Oh well," says Alana.

"And did I tell you . . . ?"

That is how, when Armend Latifi returns to the kitchen, he finds his sous-chef and line cook cooing at each other like a pair of dyspeptic pigeons.

"Toworktoworktowork!" he growls. "We have a cake to bake."

Chapter Fifty-One

Sold!

"THAT WAS FAST," MADDIE SAYS. "WHAT HAPpened?"

"So I called the restaurant," Dini says.

"Was it him? Did he steal it? Did you confront him? Was he stunned?"

Dini shakes her head. "I didn't talk to him," she says. "I talked to Alana. And no, he didn't steal it."

"What do you mean? Who did? Did you find out? Can we get it back?" Maddie must be feeling better. Sleuth stuff has revived her.

Dini looks at the floor. She looks at Maddie's orthopedic shoe. She looks out the window and sees Brenna getting off her bike. She's coming to the door. She's going to ring the doorbell.

"It's been sold," Dini says.

Chapter Fifty-Two

Terribly Sorry

"WHAT HAPPENED TO YOU?" BRENNA SAYS upon seeing Maddie slumped on the sofa with her foot propped up. "Whoa! Guess you won't be dancing, huh?"

"Not me," says Maddie.

"Uh-oh," says Brenna, doing a distressed handstand. "Now what do we do?"

"I don't know," Dini says. She tells Brenna about the passport, which Ollie found for sale on the Internet, and how he tracked the person down who was selling it, and that person yelled at him, which was not at all good for Ollie's self-confidence, and anyway, the passport's sold.

"Well, that's that," says Brenna. "Nothing more we can do." Which is true, but not very helpful.

"You guys," Maddie says, trying to fix her pillow and sending it toppling to the floor instead, "will just have to do the dance without me."

"If we can make it work," says Brenna briskly.

"You're better off on your own," Maddie says. "I wasn't that great anyway."

"You were fine," Dini protests.

It's true, she thinks. Maddie was fine. Well, she was mostly fine. A small pang of guilt turns inside Dini and prods her sharply.

"Oh, come on, Dini," says Maddie. "You know I'm a klutz."

"How are we going to do it without you?" wails Dini.

"It's one thing to dance for fun," Maddie says. "But this performance stuff—that's different."

"Look, I know it won't be the same," says Brenna, "but I do know the steps."

"I know them too, but that's not enough," Dini says. Which may be true, but it sounds mean. Did she mean to be mean? She didn't and she did, all at once. No-no-no, yes-yes!

"Oh, forget it," says Maddie.

Brenna looks hurt.

"Forget what?" says Dini. "The dance?"

"Whatever," Maddie says, and closes her eyes.

"She doesn't mean that," Brenna says.

Maddie opens one eye. "I do too," she says.

"Maddie," says Brenna, "I'd be feeling sorry for myself too if I broke my toe."

"I am *not* feeling sorry for myself!" exclaims Maddie, and now both her eyes are wide open. "Anyway, who cares?"

And that is when Dini loses it. "It's not about who's a great dancer or not, Maddie!" she cries. "This is not a competition. It's about doing stuff together. Don't you get it? And doing something for Dolly for the opening. That was the whole point, and now it's all fallen apart."

Maddie glares at Dini. "It's not my fault I broke my foot," she says.

"Toe," Dini says. "It was only a toe." What is she saying? What does she mean to say? Why can't she stop herself? It's bad enough she has to *think* mean little thoughts. Does she have to say them out loud, too?

"It's part of my foot, isn't it?" Maddie says, and snaps her eyelids shut. Exit Maddie, for all practical purposes.

"Well," says Brenna. "I guess there isn't going to

be a dance, so I'll just go on home." Exit Brenna.

Dini is sorry, so terribly sorry. For what she said and what she didn't say. And for herself. In fact, she is about up to her ears in sorriness when the doorbell rings.

Chapter Fifty-Three

Hard to Believe

DINI IS GRATEFUL TO BE OUT OF THAT ROOM with the bad feelings swirling around. She runs to the front door and peers through the peephole. And she stops. Looks again. And again.

She's heard about people who have trouble believing their eyes. She's never quite understood the concept. If you see something, it's there, surely. What's all the fuss about not believing your eyes? Belief is about things you can't see, isn't it?

Now, through that peephole, she sees who just rang the doorbell. She sees who's standing on the recently painted green-and-silver steps of Maddie's house. She sees a whole lot of people right behind that person.

The doorbell rings again, and again. Dini has recognized that fabulous face, of course, even in the fish-eye view through the peephole. Yet she finds her logical mind doing a double take, and she herself is doing what she thought was impossible. Refusing to believe her eyes.

It's Dolly! The real Dolly, not a movie image, not some made-up idea of heroes and rescues and dances through tea-gardens. Not that there's anything wrong with those, but this is really real.

"I got it!" she calls to Maddie's mom, who has emerged from her office room with an inquiring look. "It's Dolly!"

Dolly is thrilled with the steps "Glorious!" she exclaims. "Specially for me?" She enters, follows Dini in. Then she spots Maddie. "Haddie!" cries Dolly. "Dini's dear papa rang to tell us about your terrible, terrible accident. I was so upset and unsettled to hear about it! So I said to Chickoo at once, I said, 'Chickoo, my dearest, never mind all our other commitments. The press conference, the plans for the opening, the photo op at the embassy. We must drop everything we're doing and go at once to see this poor, dear girl.' Didn't I say that, Chickoo?"

"You did, Dolly," says Chickoo.

"It's Maddie," Dini says.

"Of course, that's what I said." Dolly plants a smacking great kiss on Maddie's forehead. "So unfortunate. You poor, dear child. What a crying shame to be so felled by fate!"

"It was a backpack, actually," Maddie murmurs, but she's grinning. In fact, she can't stop grinning. She's cheered up really fast. She doesn't even seem to mind Dolly mangling her name.

"Thank you for coming to see me," Maddie says.

"My delight," says Dolly. It's a lovefest.

Dolly bears treats. To be precise, Soli Dustup is carrying the box. He sets it down on the couch. He unties the ribbon (green and silver, naturally). He lifts the lid. "Have a go, dear young ladies," he says, waving his hands gleefully. "Just a few samples from my good friend Chef Latifi. He has settled on that one for the final cake." He jabs at a luscious-looking confection, a perfectly moist square topped by a single red rose petal.

Good friend? When did that happen? Never mind, it's a sight, as Dad would say, for a sore-eyed cowboy. The best part is that Dini was the one who asked the angry chef to bake that cake, and she doesn't even care that no one knows it but Maddie and Brenna. She's so happy she feels like dancing.

But there's Maddie. She's been felled. She can't dance. Dini looks at Maddie. Maddie looks back.

Then Dini offers her hand in a combination high five and pinkie clutch, their secret signal since second grade, and if it's kiddish now that they're both older, so what? Slowly, in a movement of forgiving and starting over, Maddie's hand rises to meet Dini's.

"Have some cake," Dini says.

Maddie hesitates. Then she says, "Dini, could you go to the kitchen and call Brenna? Her number's on the fridge."

"Sure," says Dini. She's on it before anyone can say "chan-chan-chan."

Brenna's brother answers the phone. He says she's not back yet, but yeah, he'll tell her as soon as she gets home. Sure, he promises. He'll say it's urgent and it's all good and Dolly's here and she, Brenna, should turn right around and go back, no problem, and of course he can remember all that, duh!

When Dini returns to the family room, the cake samples are being passed around. Judging from the murmurs of delight, they are all delicious.

That is when an idea zips through the universe and lands smack-dab in Dini's mind. "The reception," she says. "Let's ask Chef Armend to cater it. I know it's short notice, but if anyone can do it, he can. We can get Mr. Mani to e-mail him recipes if we need to, or he can make up his own."

A slow smile spreads over Soli's face. "Missy," he says, "you are a fine one for thinking on your feet. I'll phone pronto, phuttaphut, this very minute."

He pulls out his cell phone, while the rest of the

company immerse themselves in a happy haze of chocolate. Soon Soli rejoins them to announce that the subplot of the catering dilemma has come to a fine resolution. Soli's called the chef. The chef agreed. Soli then called that nice military man at the museum and told him it's all done, not to worry about a thing.

Applause breaks out. Dini's good idea has been taken seriously and carried out into the world. What could be better than that?

When the cheers have died down, Dolly says, "I, too, have a joyful announcement to make." She lobs a merry string of beads into the air. "I had a little chat with the gentleman at the museum. He's . . . you know, scatterbrained. He misunderstood my intention completely. Anyway, we agreed, of course there will be no elephant inside the museum. 'My dear sir,' I said to him, 'no problem, aise bhi problem hai kya? Let's hold the dance outside.'"

"Dance?" say Dini and Maddie together, just as Brenna reenters the scene, hot and out of breath.

"Did someone say 'dance'?" says Brenna.

"Dolly," says Maddie. "I can't dance. I've broken my toe. I know it's only a small bone, but still. . . ."

"That's right, no dancing," Maddie's mom chimes in.

"I know that," Dolly says, retrieving a ring from the folds of her sleeve. "But I've been thinking about it. Mulling and meditating, conjecturing and considering. And I have come to a conclusion."

She looks around to make sure she has everyone's attention. She needn't worry. They're riveted.

"Easy," says Dolly, throwing her arms wide in her uniquely glittery way. "Now that the dance is outside, Mini and I will join you girls."

It is too bad that Dini's dad is not present, or he would surely be slack-jawed with surprise. As it is, Dini is now unable to believe her ears.

Chapter Fifty-Four

The Not-a-Parade Parade

ANOTHER DAY WHIRLWINDS PAST, AND HERE it is, Tuesday, the day of the grand opening.

Dad remains a little bewildered, but that is because he was fixing satellite dishes on people's roofs and therefore missed much of the action. Dini has to fill him in on the dance, which is going to be simply dazzling, and the delicious cake, which Dini's sorry he missed sampling but he'll soon get a slice of the real thing. She gives him the catering update. She tells him that Maddie will be in charge of a pair of silver rosewater sprinklers. And then she lays out the still-unfolding story of Ollie and the passport.

Dad does get most of it, although he keeps asking a few questions over and over, like "Who's Mini again?" and "What's Ollie got to do with Dolly's passport?"

Speaking of Ollie, here he is with the first batch of refreshments.

"Wonderful," says Dolly, who's helping the Smithsonian staff to oversee the setup.

Ollie is hollow eyed from having chopped and stirred and baked for a whole day and some of the night, too. "Could I . . . talk to you?" he asks Dolly.

"Certainly," says Dolly. "I love to talk to fans."

Ollie shuffles his feet. Dini comes to his help. Someone has to, or he'll be standing there all day shifting from one foot to the other. "It's about your passport," Dini prompts.

Dolly gives the shuffling young man a sharp look. "Are you the culprit?" she demands.

"No!" says Ollie, galvanized. "It's a film magazine's website. They're in India. They even tweeted about auctioning off stuff."

"Filmi Kumpnee?" cry four voices together. Dini and Maddie, of course. And Dolly. And Soli Dustup.

"Those turnip heads," says Mr. Dustup. "I'll . . ." He shakes his fist. "I'll make them sorry. How dare they?" His face turns many shades of purple in quick succession. "I'll turn them upside down and inside out. I'll . . ." His ears waggle fiercely.

But Dolly is staring at Ollie in admiration. "You are a hero," she says.

"I am?" says Ollie.

"Yes, yes. You tracked my passport down. You found out who has it. You risked life and limb. . . ."

"Well," Ollie demurs. "It wasn't that dangerous or anything."

"Don't you worry," says Dolly. "We will deal with those villainous people who are trying to—what do you say in America?—make a quick buck off a stolen passport? A passport that would have been auctioned off for charity if I had my way."

"You and me," Soli says. "We'll deal with them together, Dolly darling. They'll be sorry they tangled with us."

"Hurryhurryhurry!" roars a voice, and Ollie hurries. But it is no longer a panicked hurrying.

Officially, this gathering might not be billed as a parade, but really, what else can we call it? A procession of people (and one elephant) all dressed up for the occasion. The elephant all by herself could turn such a collective walk into a parade.

Maddie has been installed in a place of honor in

a small painted gazebo that sits on the sweeping sidewalk in front of the Sackler complex, with a strategic view of both street and garden. "Here, take these." Dolly hands Maddie a pair of silver, vaselike containers with round bottoms, long tapering necks, and little sprinkler holes in their screw-top caps. "This is to welcome all our guests."

From her place in the gazebo Maddie gets to sprinkle passersby with cool, refreshing droplets of rose water. A museum staff person stands by with jugs of the magical liquid, ready to fill those sprinkler vases whenever they empty. The sparkling showers of rose-scented water make little kids giggle and run back for more.

Gretchen arrives, having taken Chef Armend and his luscious chocolate cake with rose petals to the delivery entrance and seen them safely into the building. "How exciting," she says, tapping her feet as loudspeakers begin to play Dolly songs over an outdoor PA system especially set up for the purpose.

Tourists come up to get their pictures taken with Dolly and Mini—and with Maddie in her silver-and-green skirt with a sparkly bindi on her forehead and those rosewater sprinklers in her busy hands.

"How's your toe?" her mom asks her.

Maddie shrugs and grins. "Well," she says, "it's still stuck to the rest of me, so I can't complain."

"Can we get you something?" Dini asks.

"Nope, I'm great," Maddie says. And she is. She surely is.

Tariq Hasan has brought his wife and their twins, a boy and a girl, Karim and Kamila. He has also brought along his friend Dave, and Dave's wife and their furry dog, which is the size of a small pony. "What kind of dog is that?" Brenna asks.

"A goldendoodle," says Dave's wife. "Her name's Peony. She loves to dance."

"She goes to Active Dogs Dance School," says Dave. "Just watch her when the music starts." They are proud dog parents. Peony waggles her tail; her big, square body shakes and her eyes disappear beneath her doggy bangs.

What a crowd has gathered for this occasion! Old friends and a host of new friends, new fans, all joined by their shared enthusiasm. Busloads have arrived from New York and New Jersey and North Carolina, Michigan and Ohio. Contingents

from Texas and California. There are even a few Canadian Dolly fans bearing signs like WE ♥ DOLLY IN TORONTO and I'M LOONY FOR DOLLY.

Here are other guests from the Promenade Hotel, hailing from Australia and Nigeria, El Salvador and Italy, Japan and Malawi. The hotel staff have told them all about this grand occasion, so they have dumped their plans for the day to join in. Here is the hotel manager, smiling and waving.

The fans all talk and laugh and sing Dolly songs.

The music fades and it is time for Mini to take the stage, or rather the sidewalk. A big brass gong has been set up near the garden entrance. Kris hands Mini a striker. Mini holds it in her trunk and—*bing-bing-bling!*—she hits that gong. *Bing-blong, bing-blong!*

"Oh my gosh!" Brenna cries. "Isn't that the song from the movie?"

It is, it is. Haan-haan-haan, nahin, nahin!

"Stunning!" Dini cries.

"So beautiful and talented also!" Dolly cries as camcorders shoot video and cameras click.

Mini flicks her ears, whisks her tail, and plays that gong, *bing-bing-bling!*

And here come more people. The chef hurries to

join in the festivities, having set up the refreshments inside to his satisfaction. Ollie and Alana are here. Here is Mr. Bayan, marching smartly out to welcome everyone on behalf of the Smithsonian Institution. Here is his secretary, tapping her feet in anticipation. What a grand opening dance this will be.

Chapter Fifty-Five

The Grand Opening Dance

DAD IS WAVING THE PHONE AT DINI. "FOR YOU!"

It's Mom. "Hi, my sweetoo," says Mom. "I know your dance is about to start, but I just wanted to give you the great news."

"News?" says Dini. "What news?"

"I got a call from that movie magazine you love so much," Mom says.

"Filmi Kumpnee?"

"Yes, they're giving the clinic fifty thousand rupees from the proceeds of a sale they had on the Internet. Some kind of auction. They mentioned Dolly's name, so I figured you'd want to know."

"Oh," says Dini faintly. The elegant buildings of the Freer-Sackler museum complex begin to shimmer in front of her eyes, and for a moment she wonders if she's dreaming. But Mom is going on and on about how lovely it is to know that her daughter, of whom she is so proud, is part of such a wonderful charitable drive. "And you know," says Mom generously, "I told Daddy this as well. Maybe we've misjudged your interest in all this movie non—business, Dini. Anyway, I have to go, it's very late here, but I just wanted to let you know."

Is that Dini's sensible doctor mother, now blowing kisses through the phone connection? She's making Dini feel heroic! Dini hands the phone back to Dad, who is also congratulating her, and if she doesn't duck out of reach, in a minute he'll be rumpling her hair and calling her baby names out of sheer pride.

She runs to Dolly, and who's this, also hurrying toward the star with microphone in hand? "Roopa Dalal," the woman says, stopping by the gazebo to take a breath and get sprinkled by Maddie. "I'm from the 'News 'n' Views' column of *Filmi Kumpnee.* Am I too late? Is the grand opening dance over? Is there any hope I might get an exclusive with Dolly?"

"*Filmi . . .*?" says Mr. Dustup, turning three shades of green. "Array, yaar, how dare you? Why, you—you are . . . shameproof!" He is incensed. He is outraged. He sputters. He waves his hands. "Sell Dolly's belongings for profit and then show up for an interview! I have half a blinking mind to call the police. The FBI! Why not? This is America."

Roopa is protesting and trying to say something. "Auction," she's saying. "For charity. Dolly said okay, I promise you." But Soli Dustup's a human flash flood and he roars on, regardless.

"Mr. Dustup! Stop, stop!" Dini cries. To her surprise, he stops. So does everyone else. All eyes are on Dini, and that is a lot of eyes.

"Tell us, Roopa," Dini says, and Roopa does. *Filmi Kumpnee* called Dolly to ask permission to put the passport on auction, along with a bunch of other starry artifacts, as a benefit for charities designated by the star herself. That's the truth.

Dini's mind is dancing around this new information. Of course. Dolly must have picked Mom's clinic because she knows it and she opened the new wing and all. And that's what Dolly was talking about on the phone that evening when Dini and Maddie were running down to the restaurant to order dinner.

"We were there when you took that call," she says.

"We just didn't get it, and you were so tired you weren't really paying attention."

"Anything can happen," says Dolly, "and you know, it often does."

"And then when Ollie got on Twitter, he didn't get it either; he just got scared." Misunderstanding piled on misunderstanding. Dini explains it all. It has only just become clear to her.

Slowly Mr. Dustup's face returns to its normal color. Slowly Roopa relaxes. "I was trying to tell you. We at *Filmi Kumpnee* are Dolly's loyal fans," she says. "We would never steal anything from such a good and generous star."

Only one thing remains to be clarified. "Who bought the passport?" Dini asks. "I mean, that was a lot of money."

Everybody looks at Roopa. She grins back. "Fans," she says. It turns out that a group of Dolly's fans formed a club. "I think you may know some of them—friends of yours from Swapnagiri. They all pitched in. Took it to Facebook, and then it totally went viral. Thousands of people gave a little bit. Together they made it a very lively auction, I can tell you."

"A blinking grassroots movement," says Mr. Dustup, dazed by this news. "And where's the passport now?"

"I know!" Dini cries. "It's gone to some art collection or museum, hasn't it? That's what they meant in that post on the *Filmi Kumpnee* website." She explains how that post and a backpack combined to make Maddie fall down the stairs. She ends, "So what was the big plan? What was that collection?"

Roopa beams. "Mr. Dustup," she says. "The passport and a few other Dolly-dazzling objects are on their way to the Bolly-Dazzle Museum. A gift from her loving fans."

"Array, that is phenomenal news!" cries Mr. Dustup. "I am thunderstruck and wonderstruck. Not to mention starstruck, of course." He blows an affectionate kiss to Dolly, who waves and smiles as the photographers click away.

Everyone cheers and applauds. Then, "Dance, mere saathiyon!" Dolly cries. She's calling Dini and Brenna. They run to her side, her friends and fans, to dance with her.

While the music plays and Mini beats the gong, Dolly leads them into the opening movements of the dance. They circle and circle and zigzag and circle, out from the center and back again. Haan-haan-haan, nahin-nahin! It is a grand extravaganza of a dance, with flags waving for every country where Dolly's ever been.

The whole crowd falls in, hundreds of them by now, all loving the beat. People from all over the map, some of them waving their own flags. An

enterprising vendor passing by on Constitution Avenue now hastens to the scene with his little cart of flags (Peace the World Together: Buy Flags Now) and sets up a brisk business.

Dad is dancing, and he's invited a bunch of people from the B&B. Gretchen's dancing, waving at Maddie, who's waving back with rosewater drizzles.

Even Mr. Bayan of the Smithsonian is executing

a brisk little step all his own. Tariq and his family dance too, the twins mirroring each other. And Peony the goldendoodle joins in with her owners. Waggling her big, furry body, she trots and tumbles in time to the rhythm. She follows Brenna's moves, weaving in and out right behind her and making everyone laugh. And that is not all. There are refreshments to come.

Chapter Fifty-Six

Yes-Yes-Yes, No-No!

THE MUSIC IS ON IN THE GARDEN ON THIS fine spring break Tuesday evening. Tables groan with delicacies. The company throngs among them.

"Everyone say 'Hey, Dolly!'" commands Roopa Dalal, the *Filmi Kumpnee* reporter. Her camera *click-clicks.* "The photos will be up on the website very soon," she promises. "Along with the clinic donation announcement."

"So . . . you found the passport!" Dini says.

"I did," says Roopa. "And I called Dolly at once."

"You did?" Dolly says, surprised.

"Yes. I even offered to bring it to you. But you said not to bother you! 'Auction it,' you said."

"Oh," Dolly says. "I didn't realize—it was the passport? Oh dear, how very confusing. Well, it's all fine now, isn't it? That's the important thing."

Yes, all is explained. All is understood. "If I'd

only refreshed the page," Ollie mourns. "I'd have seen the updates. I just got—"

"A little confused," says Alana, shaking her head fondly at him and making his ears turn pink.

Dad says, "If you're hunting for cougars, you start to see them in every canyon," which confuses even those who'd begun to get the bigger picture.

"He's just that way," Dini explains when Brenna looks puzzled. "He can't help it."

Of course, Armend Latifi has catered the event. It's true that his smiles may be taken for aggression by those not in the know, but the well informed can see how happy he is.

Ollie and Alana serve the canapés and pakoras, fine cheeses, and curry puffs. Some of these recipes have come zinging around the world to the chef at Dolly's request, courtesy of the baker Mr. Mani from that dreamy little town of Swapnagiri. Armend has accepted them graciously and added his own touches.

And oh yes, yes! Just look at that fountain in the center of the table, its spouts pouring rose petal milk shakes into the cups of those with fine taste.

Dini takes a plate of goodies over to Maddie, who

can hobble around in her wide, flat shoe, but her foot hurts when she's tired, so she's sitting down now. They share curry puffs and little crackers with spicy dips, crispy pakoras with potatoes and onions and cheese. Naturally, every single dish is enhanced by a dash of chocolate.

"Where's the cake?" Dad asks.

"Patience," Dini tells him.

The cake will soon be ceremonially topped by the chef himself. Armend Latifi will apply its final garnish of fresh pink and red rose petals.

Brenna turns cartwheels between the moongates.

Then, "Who's that?" Maddie says.

Dini wheels around to look. Who are these people in uniform? Wait, no. They're not in uniform, not unless you count identical black suits and sunglasses.

"Is there a problem?" Ollie asks.

"Should we whisk Miss Dolly away to a safe place?" Tariq inquires.

"Hope they're not taxwallas," Soli mutters.

This is when the yes-yes-yes of the evening turns rapidly to no-no. It takes a choreographer of dances and a lover of fillums to see this turning point coming. Chef Armend is heading for the table, bearing a bowl filled with pink and red petals. He is intent on the ceremonial decoration of the cake that will honor his Nona. The suited people are heading for Dolly, who is standing by the table.

These suited people are on a collision course with Chef Armend.

"Watch out!" Dini yells.

Chef Armend lets out a howl of grief and rage and tries to grab at the bowl as it slips from his hands.

Too late?

No, no. Brenna to the rescue. She springs. She leaps. She flies over a bench and sails onto the grass on the other side, stretching to catch the bowl of rose petals.

Brenna reaches. She stretches. She catches the bowl.

It does not crash to the ground. It does not scatter over the shrubbery. Rose petals fly off the top, but most of the precious cargo is saved.

"Here!" Brenna gasps. She hands the bowl back to the chef. He bows in gratitude, too overcome to speak.

"Stunning!" Maddie yells. Brenna collapses on the grass, breathless. Dini runs and hugs her.

"Array, my darlings, what a brilliant number that was!" Mr. Soli Dustup is so moved he has to wipe his eyes.

The people in uniform present an invitation to Dolly to attend the Easter Egg Roll at the White House the following week! "The president sends his apologies for the mix-up about the catering," they say. "Someone posted a message about it on the White House website, but it took a while to confirm the facts. The president hopes the catering problem was resolved."

"Perfectly," Dolly says. "Chickoo and I are doing a little trip to Hollywood after this, but we'll fit you in on our way back to India, right, darling?" Chickoo Uncle beams at her. "Next year I want you to invite this wonderful chef to the White House for your Egg Tumble." She introduces Chef Armend, who cannot stop glowering with joy.

With silver tongs the chef heaps rose petals upon his masterpiece. Dolly cuts the cake. The applause is thunderous.

As the pigeons coo the evening down, Mr. Bayan announces that the first of two showings of the fillum is now being seated, and that those who cannot get in will have to wait their turn for the next round. No one minds. It's all good. It's all Dolly.

"Come on, my darlings," says Mr. Soli Dustup, and Dolly's near and dear ones enter the museum, along with the Indian ambassador and other distinguished guests. They find their seats, Dini with Maddie on one side and Brenna on the other.

The projector buzzes on. The movie lights flicker onto the screen. Happy sighs float up from the audience as they settle in to watch *Kahan Hai Sunny Villa?* or *Where Is Sunny Villa?* KHSV for short. Dini catches Dad beaming at her when he should be looking at the screen. Dolly and Chickoo Uncle smile at each other. Ollie and Alana do likewise.

How fine it is to watch a great movie with true friends and fans. The journey to bring *Sunny Villa* here to Washington has taken some strange turns, but this grand opening was worth every tense moment. Now Dini can see those moments for what they were. Change. That's what. When yes turns to no and back again, or new to old and then to new once more.

Change makes people panicky. Change shimmers

up the line between life and the movies before it settles back into the next new reality. But dealing with change is not so hard, really. All a slightly heroic person has to do is help out, watch out, and take the dance one step at a time.